CONTROL FREAKS

CONTROL FREAKS

J.E. Thomas

LQ

LEVINE QUERIDO

Montclair | Amsterdam | Hoboken

This is an Arthur A. Levine book
Published by Levine Querido

LEVINE QUERIDO

www.levinequerido.com · info@levinequerido.com
Levine Querido is distributed by Chronicle Books, LLC
Copyright © 2023 by J.E. Thomas
All rights reserved.
Library of Congress Control Number: 2022945479
ISBN 978-1-64614-305-4
Printed and bound in China

Published in May 2023
First Printing

For Helen Yeager, Nichelle Nichols, Laura Pegram
and all those who help others thrive
and be seen. Thank you.

CHAPTER 1

Frederick Douglass Zezzmer

Question: How did I get through most of seventh grade without saying more than two words to half my classmates?
Answer: Because kids be kids, even at Benjamin Banneker College Prep, Colorado's #1 school for unusually competitive students. (That's what it says on the B-B website anyways. Except for the kids be kids part. That's 100% me.)

Other than the competition thing, B-B kids are like kids everywhere. We find our crew and stick with them. No matter what. Just like in *Lord of the Flies*. Which, for the record, I'm pretty sure was based on a true story.

Also for the record, B-B is packed with STEAMers: a.k.a., science heads, technovengers, enginerds, arts peeps, and mathatrons. There are a bunch of sportsters too, but they're only here because their parents love B-B's academics. I'm the only visionary inventor in the middle school though. And I have a puny crew. Just me and my best friend and gadget-making assistant, Huey Linkmeyer.

We usually meet in front of the auditorium at 8:10, five minutes before morning assembly. But today . . . ugh! Everything goes wrong.

"Out you go," Pops says, clicking the door locks on his SUV.

"But it's only 7:30!" I try not to whine. Now that I'm twelve, that's not cool anymore. But come on! Who dumps their kids at school forty-five minutes early?

"When I was a wide receiver for the Broncos, I would hit the field at 5:00 A.M. every day for two hours of sprints—rain, sleet, snow or shine. Nobody made me do it. The Zezzmer winning spirit got me up," Pops blares in his *Sports Recap with Elliott "EZ" Zezzmer* podcast voice. The podcast is the latest business in a post-football empire that includes Zezzmer Sports Management, EZ Route Running Private Coaching, and Succeed through Sports Inc.

"Dig deep, son," Pops continues. "Show some of that Zezzmer grit."

Yeah, so, here's the thing. I've lived in Denver my entire life, but Pops moved away when I was a baby. He came back six months ago with three things: a do-over family (my stepmother, Patrice, who still looks like an NFL cheerleader, and her fourteen-year-old son, T.W.), an autographed Denver Broncos jersey, and a surprise plan to reinvent my entire life before I get too stuck in my ways.

Unlike my stepbrother, who Pops adopted when he and Patrice got married three years ago, I don't have a lot of experience with Zezzmer grit. But I do recognize the look Pops gives me in the rearview. *Huge smile. Hard, dark eyes. A deep furrow between eyebrows that are as thick and black as mine.* It's the EZ stare. I read about it on the internet. When he played for the Broncos, Pops was the go-to receiver whenever the team was down. Until he wrecked his knee in his eighth season, the EZ stare meant he had made his mind up to score. He wasn't going to let anyone get in his way.

Great. I open the door a tiny bit and stick my nose through the crack. An artic blast whacks me in the face. I swear my nose hairs start to freeze. "It's still cold!"

Pops swivels around and pushes the door wide open. College football rings from back-to-back Orange Bowls gleam on his thick, dark brown fingers. He tilts his head and gives me an EZ Zezzmer-style wink. If he knew me better, he'd know I never wink.

"It's almost fifty degrees, Doug," Pops says. "Know what? We should start running together. It'll toughen you up before you start Elite Juniors this summer. Early morning runs will be fun. I'll talk to your mother." He gives me a little push then pulls the door closed when I'm out of the car. "Have a good day, son!

And then he's off, blazing down the road with family 2.0. They have to get all the way back across town to reach T.W.'s school, Northeast Denver High, by 8:00.

At least Patrice waves and says bye. T.W. just pouts. He's as sports-obsessed as Pops, which explains why he goes to a school with a dozen state championship trophies, and I go to a school that doesn't have one. Whenever I spend weekends with Pops, detours to B-B—to drop me off first on Mondays—always make T.W. mad. He slaps on his shades and glares at the high school part of B-B's campus the whole time he's here. T.W. has to be the worst stepbrother in history. Just another reason that I rather stay with *my* family:

Moms, and my stepdad since forever, Julius Jordan.

My fingers tingle like I've got a thousand paper cuts by the time I slog from the drop-off lane to the auditorium. My glasses are fogged up too. I could go inside—student IDs can open the auditorium doors thirty minutes before assembly—but I hang tough. I've seen enough horror movies to know that walking into an empty building alone is never a good idea.

"Yo, Doug!" Huey roars around the corner at 7:55. When I texted that I had to come to school early, Huey convinced his mom to bring him early too. He looks like he ran all the way from his car. His face is almost as red as his hair.

Now that he's here, I slap my student ID against the card reader, shove the door open with my pathetic, half-frozen hands and barrel into the lobby. I've never been so glad to be inside in my life.

You'd think with three hundred empty chairs to choose from, Huey and I would have a tough decision to make, but nope. We always sit in the same seats and the same row for morning assembly. Seat 1 and seat 2, row JJ. It's the designated neutral zone between the bigger crews. We sink into our chairs, then do the short version of our secret shake: two fist bumps, a finger snap, high five, low five, hand slap on the Black side (me) and the White side (him), two elbow taps, a forehead bomp, and a nod.

"Dude, it's the first day after spring break. Why'd we have to get here so early?" Huey asks. He says *we* even though I'm the one who didn't have a choice.

I roll my eyes. "Blame T.W. His school counselor called on Saturday and told Pops and Patrice to come in early today. It's probably some huge mess with his grades again."

Huey squints at me. "Being around your dad and T.W. is aging you, man." He jabs a thumb at my Afro. "I think your hair's going grey!" He snorts. "Did you at least make progress with"—he checks to make sure nobody snuck in the auditorium in the last two seconds—"Operation DazzleYee?"

"I wish." Figuring out how to impress our principal, Dr. Yee, is my top priority this term. But having the best grades in my class, doing a ton of extra credit, and presenting one of my best inventions—the DougApp Virtual Buddy personal assistant and homework helper—at the science fair haven't budged the needle yet.

If I'm going to be the first middle schooler ever picked to represent B-B at Rocky Mountain GadgetCon, Operation DazzleYee has to be huge. I was supposed to spend last weekend making a surefire plan. Guess who held me back.

"Don't let it bug you," Huey says. "Jest bests stress."

I stare at him. "Jest bests stress? What does that even mean?"

Huey shrugs. "I dunno. Be happy instead of freaked out, maybe? It's one of the things Grandpa used to say." He pulls a deck of cards from his shirt pocket and slaps it on the armrest. He's always practicing new tricks to show residents at Porch View, the assisted living center where his grandfather used to stay. Huey's so good that

6

the manager at Porch View wants him to do a big show for everybody. Huey keeps saying no, because he has chronic stage fright. The only people he's comfortable performing for are the senior citizens on his grandfather's old floor, and me.

I cut the deck the way he taught me. First time in half. Second time in thirds. Third time in quarters. Then I turn away, shuffle the deck, and pluck out a card. It's the ten of clubs. I sneak the card back and snag a different one. Card #2 is the jack of diamonds.

"Jack of diamonds," Huey says the second I turn back. "And the first card you pulled was the ten of clubs." He blinks. "Was I close?"

I catch myself mid-eye roll. Huey hardly ever makes a mistake. But he still panics at the big finish. "I wasn't close, was I?" His eyebrows twitch. "Where did I mess up? Gimme a sec. I'll take notes."

"If by close you mean nailed it, then yeah. You were close." I rub my hands together. I'm ready for another trick, but it's already after 8:00. Other kids and teachers start piling in. Huey grabs the deck and shoves it in his pocket before anyone gets near.

We bored-clap as LaVontay Scott, a sixth-grade ballet prodigy, and the other arts peeps pirouette and fa-la-la to the seats closest to the stage. LaVontay does a bunch of leaping high kicks that he obviously practiced during spring break. Not to be outdone, Spike Weatherly starts singing opera or whatnot.

"I feel your pain about the weekend!" Huey has to shout because Charlotte Kendsierski and Spike have started having a major talent throwdown. She plays air drums and sings country; Spike dumps opera for beat-box and rap.

"My parents are"—Huey makes air quotes—" discussing their living arrangements again." He makes a face. "Do you know how weird it is to have your first mom and first dad talk about getting back together when they've already married other people—twice?"

"Nope." No worries there. "My parents are never, ever getting back together."

We hoist our knees to avoid getting trampled as the serious STEM kids pollinate the chairs behind the arts peeps and the sportsters swarm the back rows. Almost everybody has the post–spring break blues so they're still half asleep. But a few of the mathatrons are having some kind of verbal algebra tournament. They hurl half-finished equations at each other like spears.

"You know how Grandpa taught me a new set of card tricks every time one of my original parents got married?" Huey says. "I counted them up this weekend after my parents told me their news." He shakes his head. "I know a lot of card tricks, man. I have six parents to manage, counting the steps. They stress me out. Nobody's got it as bad as me in the parent department."

"Wanna bet?" I didn't expect to compete in Whose Parents Are Worse? when I came to school this morning, but this is B-B. Most of us compete in everything. There must be something in the air.

"At least all of your folks have always been around," I remind him. I tick off points on my hand, starting with my thumb. "One: Pops got hurt right after I was born. Two: He didn't get the coaching job he wanted so he flew to LA faster than Superman to be a commentator on ESPN. Three: He said he left us behind because Moms was finishing graduate school and I was in day care, but I think it's really because we would've been in the way. Four: He was only supposed to be gone a year or two, but 'new opportunities' kept coming up. And five: He shows up at my twelfth birthday party and acts like being gone most of my life doesn't matter. Then he tries to take over!" I make a fist and pump the air. Boom. I'm the winner.

"Not so fast, man." Huey's probably the only kid at B-B who doesn't like serious contests, but this is just us. It's safe. He's obviously getting into this game. He makes his own fist. "First off, you lose a point because your pops was here in spirit. You always got birthday and holiday gifts. And you said your mom always got a check on the first of the month to help take care of you."

Huey drops his little finger and waggles the remaining four digits at me before starting to count his parent grievances on his other hand. "Now for me. One: All of the grownups in my family still act like parents, even after they get divorced. Two: They hardly agree on anything. Three: They each have, like, three thousand rules—and they're all different. And four, I have to schlep my stuff to a different house every other week. I'm just a regular kid, Doug. Trying to keep track of what I'm supposed to do where is hard." He does jazz hands. "It's a tie, dude!"

"You forgot about Pops's online classes." I smirk. Pops figures if he can fast-learn a bunch of sports-related businesses after spending most of his career on the field, he can fast-learn hands-on parenting. He's taking classes by some guy named Greg G. at The Power Parenting Group. Thanks to Greg G., Pops has opinions about everything. *What I eat. When I sleep. Where I live and go to school. What I'm going to be when I grow up.* The list goes on and on. It wasn't bad when he lived in LA. But now he has a fancy new house in a Denver suburb called Highlands Ranch. He's forty minutes from my home in Park Hill—an older neighborhood in the middle of the city—but he's still close enough to want to oversee everything.

He doesn't care that Moms raised me her way for most of my life. Or that she got remarried when I was two. Nothing makes Pops launch into his "There are no ex-parents, only ex-spouses" speech faster than when people think Julius is my original dad, because we have the same Afro (his is shorter), the same black glasses (his are thicker), the same smirky laugh (mine is smirkier), and we both like tech. Julius has been around for as long as I can remember, but that doesn't stop Pops from pressing me to be less like Julius and more like him. Greg G. says kids can only have one dad.

Huey's face falls. Greg G.'s online classes are the tie-breaker. Not that it's a prize I actually want or anything, but award the winning point in the Headaches from Parents Olympics to me.

"Sorry to rub it in, but there's more." I pause for effect. "Pops wants me to do Elite Juniors sports camp this summer. He announced it at dinner last night."

"No way! Doesn't he know GadgetCon is this summer?!"

"He doesn't care. You know how he is. Pops says inventing is a hobby. He wants me to focus on sports."

It doesn't matter that winning GadgetCon before I turn thirteen is part of my fifty-seven-step strategy to become the World's Greatest Inventor. Or that individuals can't enter GadgetCon: contestants have to be nominated by their schools.

"Pops says there's no guarantee Dr. Yee will choose me for GadgetCon. But since his company is sponsoring Elite

Juniors this year, getting into summer sports camp is a sure thing. He says I should be grateful for "—I make air quotes—"this amazing opportunity."

I can count on Moms to put her foot down about me changing schools, or playing tackle football, or spending more time on sports than I spend studying, but even she doesn't get how important GadgetCon is. She says Pops and I need to find common ground and learn to compromise. Translation: It's up to me to change Pops's mind about GadgetCon.

When it comes to Elite Juniors sports camp, I can't just say no.

CHAPTER 2

Frederick Douglass Zezzmer

"O of! I heard about Elite Juniors. It's run by former pro athletes. It's supposed to be tougher than Marine Corps boot camp." Huey shuffles an imaginary deck of cards and grinds his teeth. "It's going to be awful. No offense, Doug, but you suck at sports."

"True." Though I could be a lot better if I wanted to. I smoke Julius at hoops whenever we play. But that's just for fun. Not everybody wants to be a serious athlete, even if they can.

"Heads down!" Huey jabs me just in time. He yanks an emergency glob of papers from his pocket. I whip out the inventor's notebook that Julius gave me and pretend to sketch with my thumb. All around us, kids check their phones, tie their shoelaces, or pretend to be asleep. Nobody makes eye contact with the two girls prowling the aisles scoping for empty chairs.

Travis Elizabeth Cod (a.k.a. The Shark) and Padgett Babineaux are the only kids without a crew. The Shark is a nine-year-old, grade-skipping brainiac who trudges through middle school with lopsided dreadlock ponytails and a book-stuffed backpack almost as big as she is.

And all I'll say about Padgett is that she's super intense, even for an eighth grader. When she was in third grade, she swore she wouldn't cut her hair until she won the Nobel Prize in Physics. Now she's got blond hair down to her knees. No joke.

"Whoa—did you see that?" Huey asks. He pokes me as Padgett clomps past our row in her regular uniform of a faded B-B sweatshirt, baggy overalls, and sky-blue clogs. "The technovengers were trying to keep The Shark from sitting with them, but she totally faked them out. I think . . ."

BONK! Huey breaks off when a laminated student ID card smacks the top of his head. *BONK. BONK. BONK.*

"Yo, dweebazoids. This is sportster space. No one said you could talk around us. Shut up."

The voice is unmistakable. It's Ritchie "The Enforcer" Nichols, the biggest kid in middle school. If Ritchie's behind us, that means Farrow McLeod, the eighth-grade sportster king, is too. Unrequested eye contact with Farrow is forbidden. Initiating conversation is death.

We don't *have* to turn around, but we can't help ourselves. Farrow's daily hair gel experiments defy description. We have to see what's sculpted on his head today.

The risk is totally worth it. The sides of Farrow's hair are slicked down flat. They glisten like ice rinks. The front stands up in goopy brown spikes. I can't tell what's happening in the back, but if the oily ring on his collar is any indication, it's amazing.

Farrow bares his teeth at us for daring to look at him. His braces glint like Klingon swords. His freckles have an inhuman glow. He lifts one hand slowly, like it weighs a hundred thousand pounds, then aims a finger in my direction.

Oh man . . . I'm being summoned.

BONK! This time Ritchie's ID card smacks my head. Great. I'll probably spend the entire morning with a dented Afro.

"Word's out your dad's company is sponsoring Elite Juniors's sports camp this summer," Farrow says. "It's supposed to have a lot of new pro workouts and all these club team coaches and college scouts." *BONK.* "Is that true?"

I kind of nod but mostly lean back out of Ritchie's ID card's range. "Yep."

"Cool." Farrow wipes a trickle of hair gel from his forehead. "I'll tell my parents to sign me up." He closes his eyes. Talk's over.

Ritchie turns his attention back to Huey. *BONK. BONK. BONK.* He's winding up for another bonk when someone behind him clears their throat.

"I wouldn't do that."

"Says who?" Ritchie half-turns. The blood drains from his face. "Oh . . . hey, Padgett. You found a seat. Uh, cool."

"Hey." Her voice is flat. Her eyes narrow. She grabs a wad of her Rapunzel hair and piles it on top of her head like a squirrel's nest.

For the record, B-B has a very strict no-fighting policy. It's, like, number three on a ninety-point list of don'ts or whatever. But Padgett Babineaux never has to actually fight. The threat of being Babineauxed is scary enough. Rumor is, she has black belts in three different martial arts, and supposedly somebody somewhere once saw her dismantle a LEGO castle with her teeth.

"I . . . we . . . were just joking," Ritchie sputters. He taps Farrow's head with his ID card. It comes back glistening with goo. "See? Told you. Just kidding around." The other sportsters in his row edge as far away as possible without actually leaving their seats.

"Maybe you should stop." Padgett pops out her retainer with her tongue, flips it up to drain the spit, then chomps down to put it back in place.

"Yeah. Sure. We were done anyway," Ritchie says. But he catches our eyes when he turns away from Padgett and mouths, "You're dead."

Lucky for us, Dr. Yee chooses that moment to bound down the center aisle and hop on the stage.

Good news: He doesn't have that really sad "I don't know why I thought I could save the world through teaching" look on his face today. Bad news: He's got an iPad tucked under his arm.

"Oh no . . ." I whisper.

"Word," Huey breathes.

This is Dr. Yee's first year at B-B. He's always trying new stuff and documenting the results. So far, he's changed something every month. Like making it mandatory to go to the common room for social time during free period. Or deciding we can't skip PE for robotics club anymore. Or changing the school's Wi-Fi to block videogames, movie and TV streamers, and all social media except B-B's private, supervised platform, MeU.

Dr. Yee with an iPad is never good.

"Hello, Benjamin Banneker middle schoolers!" he happy-yells. He flashes the Vulcan hand salute. "Welcome back from spring break! Did you enjoy your time off?"

A few kids clap. Somebody gurgles a tinny "Whoop." The rest of us stay quiet. In situations like this, it's best not to breathe.

Dr. Yee scans the room for the whooper. His gaze settles on Ramón Chavez, one of the technovengers. Ramón waves his arms in the universal "it wasn't me" sign, but Dr. Yee doesn't get it.

"Good for you, Ramón! Glad to hear it! Everybody, cheer for Ramón!" He gives a hearty thumbs-up as Ramón slithers down in his seat. "Now students, as you know, we traditionally jump right back into classes after spring break. But not this year!"

My neck starts to prickle. Huey's legs jerk. Padgett Babineaux click-slurps her retainer two rows back. All around us, kids mutter nervously.

"What's happening?"

"Are we having a pop quiz?"

"I bet he's going to make the GadgetCon announcement. Take a picture of me when he calls my name. I spent spring break practicing how to look surprised."

"We better not be doing a nature hike. That's all I'm saying. I'm wearing my good shoes."

"Ha! No announcements. No tests. No hikes." Dr. Yee snort-laughs a little. "I remember middle school. I remember it really well, as a matter of fact. I wouldn't drop surprises like that on you. But that doesn't mean we're not going to shake things up!" He grins at the grown-ups standing like sentries at the end of each row. The ones closest to me—Coach Judy; our homeroom and English teacher, Mr. Happy; and Mrs. Jalil, the assistant principal—fidget nervously.

Dr. Yee doesn't notice. "Students, your teachers and I are excited to announce the latest innovation to our wonderful Benjamin Banneker academic program. For the rest of the week, you're going to participate in a very special middle school competition."

"Yesssss!" I'm on my feet doing a happy dance in a second.

Huey rolls his eyes.

The sportsters aren't happy either. They like intense competitions, but most B-B events are all about STEAM. Even Dr. Yee wouldn't mess with a winning formula.

Aside from Huey and the sportsters, enthusiasm reaches a fever pitch. "Competition, yaaaah! Bring it on!" Padgett Babineaux hollers. Somebody in the enginerd section yells, "Way to start the week, Dr. Yee!" Spontaneous applause fills the auditorium. As soon as her American Sign Language interpreter shares the news, Thyme Ragland-Sanchez, a seventh-grade science head, gets the kids in her row to cheer and do the wave.

And to think today started off as a disaster. Ha! Here's my chance to impress Dr. Yee. I'm going to dominate this competition.

Dr. Yee motions for quiet. He smiles. But . . . wait. His eyes look like Pops's when he's doing the EZ stare.

"As I said, this is a very special middle school competition," Dr. Yee continues. "We call it STEAMS. And for the first time ever, sixth, seventh, and eighth graders will work on projects together. You're going to love it!"

No! No-no-no-no-no-no-NO! This shouldn't be happening. A multigrade team competition will mess up my plan. The whole point of Operation DazzleYee is to get Dr. Yee to notice *me*. Frederick Douglass Zezzmer. There's no way to stand out if I'm one of a dozen kids on a team.

I'm not the only one who feels this way. Thyme and the wavers are in shock. Some of the wavers freeze with their arms in the air. A bunch of science heads make "we just smelled farts" faces. A couple of the arts peeps pretend faint. And the chatter around me kicks into high gear.

> *"I'm allergic to team competitions."*
> *"I am NOT doing a team project with sixth graders. They're barely out of diapers."*
> *"Seventh graders are obsessed with their shoes."*

"Easy for you to say. You're in eighth grade. Your class eats the rest of us for lunch!"

Huey fake puts away his imaginary card deck and yanks out his phone. He checks to be sure he's on the school's Wi-Fi, and taps an icon.

"Don't panic," he mumbles. "It'll be okay." He tries to sound calm but I totally see sweat on his forehead.

"Listen, competitions have to have rules. Maybe Dr. Yee already posted them on MeU. I'll look."

"Forget the rules," I moan. I drop my head in my hands. My life feels like a dumpster fire right now.

But then my brain switches to desperation-level inventor mode. If I can visualize turning toothpicks, a box of spaghetti, a handful of crabapple tree leaves, and some dental floss into a compostable table fan, maybe I can invent a way to convince Dr. Yee to drop this team contest idea.

"I'm sure some of you are already trying to figure out how to get me to cancel the team competition," Dr. Yee says. I raise my head. *Is he looking at me?* "You can stand down. This contest is happening. And it starts today. Of course, it never hurts to have a little extra incentive when you're about to try something new, am I right? So, without further delay, Coach Judy and Mr. Happy, if you please—"

Coach Judy spins on her heels and runs down the aisle toward the auditorium doors. She's as fast as a racehorse. Mr. Happy's a sloth. He's only gone about twenty feet before Coach Judy is back. She wheels a cart carrying something bulky covered by a big black tarp.

"I couldn't find the rules," Huey says. Then he gets distracted. "What do you think's under the blanket? It looks like a *Law & Order* body bag." He gets excited. "Maybe it's a fake body. Maybe figuring out what happened to the fake body is the team challenge. That would be cool!" He tugs at his hair. "Unless it's a creepy looking fake body. I wonder if it's creepy looking. If it's creepy looking, I'm not down for that."

Coach Judy whips off the tarp. It wasn't covering a fake body. It was covering the largest gold trophy I've ever seen in my life. Oh wow!

Everybody starts buzzing again:

"What's that for?"

"I don't care. I want it."

"Too bad. My dads say I'm a winner so it's mine."

"I'll do a team competition if I can have that trophy."

"I thought you were allergic."

"I was. Then I saw the trophy. I'm feeling better now."

"I knew you'd be excited." Dr. Yee does a little dance on the stage. "The winning team will be an inspiration for all of us! I can't wait to see your ingenuity and inventiveness. I know I'll be impressed!"

And then I get what has to be my best idea ever. Thanks to STEAMS, my whole pathetic life just turned around. Operation DazzleYee is back in business.

My face gets hot. I start to sweat.

"Dude, are you okay?" Huey asks.

I bobblehead-nod. I don't have words because my brain is happy-screaming. The yammer around us gets louder and louder. I don't care. Huey pulls out a pen and starts scribbling on his papers. I don't look at what he's writing.

I may not know what STEAMS means—maybe science, technology, engineering, arts, and math surprise?—but that's not important.

My inventor's brain shifts to Plan B mode. The path to Rocky Mountain GadgetCon is clear. It's like a Rube Goldberg machine. A chain reaction. One step leads to another and another and another until . . . BAM!

Here's the plan:

1. Lead my STEAMS team to victory.
2. Amaze Dr. Yee with my leadership and STEAM skills.

3. Snag the coveted spot for GadgetCon—which also convinces Pops to let me skip sports camp.
4. Win GadgetCon. *Obviously!*
5. Check another box on my plan to be the World's Greatest Inventor.

STEAMS is the ticket to everything.
All I have to do is win.

CHAPTER 3

Huey Linkmeyer

I write backwards when I get nervous. It calms my nerves because I have to concentrate more than usual to make sentences that only read the right way when you hold them up to a mirror.

ꙅbɿɒwʞɔɒd ǫᴎiɈiɿw m'I ,woᴎ Ɉʜǫiɿ bᴎA
!ƎMIT ƆIᗺ

There's way, way, way too much going on. First off, Doug went from being bummed about STEAMS to being ten thousand percent all in. It took, like, half a second. I wasn't even finished cheering him up.

And second off, Dr. Yee hasn't explained the rules yet. Nobody even knows what a STEAMS competition is. It could be hard. I wonder if it's hard. I'm not good at surprises that are hard. Grandpa used to say, "risk a mess to get to yes," but he's not here to motivate me anymore. And even though they never actually say it, I'm pretty sure the one thing Mom, Dad, and the steps agree on is that it's not cool to fail.

"Here we go!" Doug yelps. "Dr. Yee's about to share some news."

Our principal taps the microphone. I don't know why he does that. The pops send lightning bolts through my ears.

"As the great Albert Einstein is believed to have said, 'Logic will get you from A to Z. Imagination will get you everywhere.' STEAMS will put your logic skills, imagination, and more to the test," Dr. Yee proclaims. "I know you're wondering exactly what STEAMS stands for. It's an acronym—an abbreviation—for all the categories you'll compete in this week. There will be contests in all the usual STEM disciplines: science, technology, engineering, and math."

Doug rubs his hands. He leans forward.

"Plus, you'll have contests in arts."

Doug makes a face. The arts peeps holler.

"Plus, drumroll please, you'll also have contests in sports."

The sportsters erupt like volcanoes. "Fiiiiiinally! A fair competition!" Farrow roars. "That's what I'm talking about!"

"Are you kidding me?" Doug moans. He sags like a popped balloon.

"I'll take questions in a minute, but first I want to explain why your teachers and I think a team event is so important right now," Dr. Yee continues. "Most of you are incredibly competitive in STEAM. You're off the charts competitive. There are literally no scales that can measure how individually competitive you are."

"That's why we win all the prizes," a mathatron yells.

"The individual prizes. And a lot. Not all." Dr. Yee gets serious. He clasps his hands behind his back and paces the length of the stage. "But you often don't do as well in team competitions. I'm sure you remember the egg drop challenge debacle in September. And my predecessor, Mrs. Alvord, told me that our entire delegation had to take a time-out during Colorado Hack-a-Thon last year. Things like that concern me. If you're going to develop scientific breakthroughs, travel to the farthest corners of the galaxy, and solve problems on Earth that previous generations couldn't fix—like climate change, inequality, and food and water shortages—you need to learn to work together, am I right?"

Doug's hand shoots up like a rocket. Dr. Yee winces. His sigh carries all the way to row JJ. Doug has a reputation for asking tough questions.

"Douglass."

"Two things," Doug says. "First, I think you should reconsider making us do sports in the competition."

Dr. Yee looks relieved. "Not a question." He shakes his head. "Next."

"I mean . . . don't you think it's wrong to make us do sports if we don't want to?" Doug asks quickly. "No matter how you spell it, there're no sports in STEM. Or in STEAM."

Some of the mathatrons start to quiet-clap.

"It's STEAM*SSSS*, Zezzmer. And there are too sports in STEAMS!" Missy-Bella Knight shouts. She holds the school record for rapid-fire knockouts in dodgeball.

"Yeah! What she said!" Farrow stomps his feet like he's leading an army platoon. "Sports! Sports! Sports!" The stomps catch on like wildfire. In a second, all the sportsters are doing it.

"There are not!" A science head does a spunky hollaback. She's a little late, but still, *yay!*

"Well, there should be! Sports! Sports! Sports!" Titus Stanley jumps up. He has ridiculous hand-eye coordination. And enough energy to run a tank. His parents have him enrolled in, like, a dozen club sports. The rumor mill says his grandpa puts cornstarch in his hair so it looks white and uses him as a ringer in senior citizen pickleball.

A bunch of musicians in the arts peeps' section try to drown out the sportsters with a chant. "Hey-hey! Ho-ho! Sports in STEAMS have got to go! Hey-hey! Ho-ho!"

Doug has started a revolution.

TWEEEEP!!

Coach Judy's whistle cuts through the air like a fire alarm. She swipes her fingers across her mouth in the universal "zip it" sign. We zip. She flips her curly gray ponytail over her shoulder and points at our chairs. Every kid except Doug sits, and even his legs buckle. Nobody messes with Coach Judy when she's in a mood.

"Thank you, Coach Judy," Dr. Yee says. "Douglass, before that . . . whatever that was . . . you asked if I thought it was wrong to make you compete in sports if you don't want to."

Doug nods.

"Good question. The answer is no. Next."

"But . . ."

"And your parents agree." Dr. Yee opens his arms like a singer hitting a glory note. "Everyone's parents agree. I sent an email last Friday. No objections from anyone." He smiles. Score: Dr. Yee, 1. Sad, put-upon, nonsportster students, 0. "Next."

"Um," Doug continues, "if we have to do sports, and if we have to be in teams, can we at least pick who's in our group?"

Dr. Yee looks pleased. "Another good question! The answer is yes . . ."

I blow out the breath I didn't even realize I was holding.

". . . and no." Dr. Yee kills my mood with two words. "Based on the data I've collected, it looks like most of you partner with the same people over and over again if you have a choice."

"There's nothing wrong with that," Ritchie mutters.

Word! I always try to partner with Doug on group projects. My body ages light-years if a teacher goes rogue and assigns the teams.

"There are over two hundred and fifty students in the Benjamin Banneker middle school. STEAMS will be a wonderful reminder of what an incredible community you are a part of—there are so many people for you to get to know," Dr. Yee says. "All you have to do is try."

Everybody groans. Grown-ups tinkering with kid cliques is always a disaster. Didn't Dr. Yee say he remembered middle school?

"After assembly, you'll head to homeroom for more details," Dr. Yee continues. "Short story: there will be fifty-one teams of five students each. Your homeroom teacher will hand out your assignments, carefully engineered to be totally random, and I hope you stick with them. But you will also have a short time to modify them if you wish." He wags a finger at us. "HOWEVER, if you choose to do this, you may not just work with kids from your own grade. Each team must have at least one sixth grader, one seventh grader, and one eighth grader. My advice is to lean into the joy of working with different people. It's so cool!" Dr. Yee bounces from one foot to the other. I've never seen him this excited. "You'll make friends with students you didn't know. You'll try new things. You'll learn to *co-op-er-ate* and *col-lab-or-ate*. Everyone must have an important role in STEAMS. And even if you don't win, you'll learn that failing can be fulfilling."

"Failure is *not* an option!" a sixth grader in a Coding Is Life T-shirt howls.

"There's a first time for everything," Dr. Yee says. "Preliminary work happens today. Elimination rounds begin tomorrow." He does another Vulcan hand salute. "It's time to get this competition started, am I right? Let's go full steam ahead for STEAMS!"

CHAPTER 4

Frederick Douglass Zezzmer

Ten minutes later, two hundred and fifty-five sixth, seventh, and eighth graders lurch out of the auditorium and stumble into the lobby.

Nobody's happy with STEAMS. The STEMers want more STEM. The arts peeps want more arts. The sportsters want all sports. Dr. Yee didn't budge on any requests. He snapped our tender young spirits like fresh tortilla chips. We're defeated and resigned to five long days of teacher-inspired pain.

Even though our futures are bleak, the usual traffic jam kicks in at the outside door as kids decide whether to layer up or layer down. The issue is Denver's fickle weather. It's like that cranky old aunt at a family reunion. The one who drags on you to eat something then swats your hand when you reach for a cookie. Moms said one year when she was a kid, it was seventy degrees in December and snowed in June. I haven't seen a summer snow yet, but I've had plenty of experience with it pouring rain when I leave in the morning, only to turn dry as a desert before noon.

Huey and I are wedged under some enginerds' stinky armpits when the kids closest to the door bellow, "It's hot now!"

For the record, I'm still recovering from trekking out of Pops's SUV this morning in sub-fifty-degree weather, so I decide to keep my jacket on no matter what.

The traffic jam starts unjamming. Everybody who has enough room to move unzips their jackets, pulls off their sweaters, and stuffs their just-in-case clothes in their backpacks.

"Maybe the competition won't be so bad," Huey says. "I'm thinking it won't be bad. In fact, I'm sure it won't be bad at all if we're on the same team." He smears his face with gobs of sunscreen, following Stepmom #2's rule about proactive skin protection.

"We're *always* on the same team." Oof. That sounded harsh. Not cool. My inventor brain starts churning. Huey isn't always so great in big competitions, especially since Grandpa Linkmeyer died, but since I'll be team leader, I can dream up a way for us to win.

"Teaming with each other is a good thing," I add quickly. "We know each other's moves." I throw some fake Captain America punches at his shoulder. Huey counters with a fake Black Panther claw swipe at my nose.

We step over a red-faced sixth grader who's turtle-flopped on her back so her friends can pull her extra pair of sweatpants over her shoes. Then we take a deep breath, elbow our way through the door, and start up the path that goes from the auditorium to the main middle school building.

Before B-B's campus was a school, it was Denver's largest urban golf course. Back then, the path was a gravel track for golf carts and maintenance trucks. Now, instead of going to the clubhouse or the driving range, the path winds all the way down to the lower school, all the way up to the high school, and off to the side for middle school.

It's not gravel anymore, either. When scientists, engineers, doctors, and teachers from around the country decided to build B-B twenty years ago, they replaced the gravel with thick, diamond-shaped pavers engraved with the names of people who used STEM to change the world. Most have names of people who lived a long time ago, but now that B-B graduates are out of college and working, some of their names are on pavers, too. Like W.

Porter Cromwell, the scientist who's developing a cure for Alzheimer's. She went here.

I leapfrog over pavers for John Glenn and Luiz Walter Alvarez. "A team STEAMS competition is going to be tough, but it's also the best way to impress Dr. Yee." I hop over pavers for Chien-Shiung Wu and Patricia Bath. "So let's look at this like we're trying to make a gadget. Zezzmer's First Law of Inventing is to clearly define the problem you're trying to solve, right?"

"Yep." Huey taps pavers for Charles Best and Marie Curie.

"Our problem is that we don't excel at sports," I use my shoe to flick the world's slowest bug off the paver for Marie Van Brittan Brown.

Huey grinds his teeth. "That's an understatement. I flunked volleyball."

"Yeah but . . ."

"Coach Judy had a panic attack when you tried out for track."

"Which proves my point that mandatory school sports should be illegal." I stop by pavers for Granville Woods and Samuel E. Blum. "But that's a fight for another day. We need to focus on getting that trophy." I sneak a side-eye at him. "Um, can you handle the arts part of the competition with your card tricks?"

Huey gulps and ducks his head. He says stage fright is like having the world's meanest bully yapping nonstop in his ear.

"Yeah so . . ." I kick a clump of dirt and send it flying. "That's all I've got." Nobody knows exactly what Dr. Yee has planned for STEAMS, but he did say everybody has to have an important role in the competition.

Huey must remember that too. "Grandpa always said, 'cheers to fears.' He said the way to get over stage fright was to find something I care about more than I care about being scared. Know what? That'll be STEAMS." He lifts his chin. "I can care about that. What's the plan?"

I drape an arm across Huey's shoulders, trying not to look as relieved as I feel. I have to win this competition. But there's no way I want to have to choose between winning and a friend.

I make a checklist in the air. "Like I said, you're good at card tricks. That's artsy and we don't need any more arts peeps to mess up our vibe. *Check!* And I'm amazing at STEM. *Check!* All we need is a sportster for sports and a couple of fillers to round out our group, then the STEAMS trophy is ours. Guaranteed."

I scan for potential teammates. Task one: Find a sportster.

It's not looking good. The sportsters swarm around each other like mosquitoes. They don't want anybody else in their space. They're excited to finally have a chance to win a schoolwide competition.

Farrow and Ritchie are obviously determined to build the ultimate all-sportster team. They're doing a walking huddle with Missy-Bella, Titus, and Pixie Stewart, a seventh-grade basketball player who's already taller than Dr. Yee. Every couple of seconds, Farrow's head pops up and he surveys the other sportsters. He's clearly still looking for winners.

Liam Murphy, an eighth grader who always lugs a duffel full of sports equipment, comes up fast on the outside. He's hauling a lacrosse stick, a football, three basketballs, a field hockey pole or whatever, and swim trunks. And he's not even sweating.

"That's who we need," I tell Huey. "We'll nail this competition with him on our team."

Liam zooms by us. "Yo, Farrow! Wait up!"

Farrow doesn't stop. He nudges his group to move faster. None of them turn around.

"Weird." I push up my glasses and rub my chin. What's the deal? Farrow's acting like he doesn't want Liam on his team. That makes no sense.

Liam comes from a whole family of athletes. His mom was on the U.S. soccer team. His dad played professional baseball before he became a superstar in competitive fly-fishing. His oldest sister runs cross country in college and his second oldest sister plays softball at T.W.'s school. Sports are in his genes, just like his bushy blond Thor hair.

We watch as Liam hops off the path and runs in the grass so he's out of the crowd. He's really moving! If that strip of grass was a field full of opposing players, they'd be shaking in their spiky shoes. Liam Murphy's a train! Liam Murphy's a rocket! Liam Murphy's . . .

"Whoa!"

I flinch as Liam hits the ground.

"How did he do that?" Huey asks. "It's like he tripped over the air."

"I'm good!" Liam scrambles around to collect his stuff. "Yo, Farrow—save me a seat in homeroom, okay? I'll see you inside." He crams his swim trunks on his head and then spider-crawls across the grass to grab a basketball before it rolls away. Farrow and his crew keep walking.

Mr. Happy is waiting for us at the entrance to homeroom alley, a section of the second floor of the main building where sliding accordion walls and three doorways have turned one huge space into separate sixth-, seventh-, and eighth-grade meeting spots.

"He beats us every time," Huey gasps when we finally reach the landing. "Those rumors about underground teacher tunnels must be true. You think they're true? They must be true because Mr. Happy is slow-slow-slow."

He's also crankier than usual. He clutches a stack of papers and stares at us sourly until the entire seventh grade forms a single straight line, kindergarten style.

"A line? Really? That's so unnecessary," Cherub Lewis grumbles. "We're not babies."

Mr. Happy must have heard her because he makes us wait another full minute before letting us in.

One.

At.

A.

Time.

"Not my fault," Cherub whines when someone reminds her of tip #5 on the secret list of how to survive middle school: Never irritate the homeroom teacher.

Mr. Happy thrusts a piece of paper at my head as soon as I reach the door. "Here are the rules for this competition. This is your only copy. Do not lose it. Do not tear it. Do not throw it away. We'll discuss the rules in more detail in a few minutes. Until then, go inside and sit quietly. No laughing, no water, no laptops, no snacks. No, you may not go to the bathroom. No, you may not move around. No, you may not use your phone. This competition is going to be marvelous. I'm sure we will all have fun. Yay."

Huey is standing right behind me so he had to hear all the instructions, but Mr. Happy peels off another sheet of paper and jabs it in his ear anyway as I walk in. "Here are the rules for this competition. This is your only copy. Do not lose it. Do not tear it. Do not throw it away . . ."

Once we're inside, Huey and I sit across from each other, four rows from the front. That's usually a safe, "out of sight, out of mind" space in homeroom.

Then, even though every single kid in the class is perfectly capable of reading the rules for ourselves, Mr. Happy tells Bucky Dillon to read them out loud.

"Umph," Bucky stares at the floor and shakes his head.

"Humor us," Mr. Happy says. He obviously doesn't know Bucky's voice is changing. Forcing him to speak is going to be torture. For us.

"Wel^llll Come to^ooo ST^E ams." Bucky's voice sounds like the combination of a metal bucket scraping the floor and a wild animal howl. "It will be^ee a ^ing maz."

"Never mind," Mr. Happy says quickly. He points at me. "Douglass Zezzmer, take over."

There are ten rules on the list. Seriously . . . ten! Why do we need ten rules for one week?

"Any day now, Douglass," Mr. Happy grunts.

I start reading. "Number one: Any teams who fail to complete a challenge will be disqualified. Number two: Any teams who do not cooperate, collaborate, and give each member an important role will be disqualified. Number three: Any teams who fail to follow directions completely will be disqualified."

My armpits start to tingle. This list says *disqualified* a lot!

"Number four: Teams who complete a challenge successfully will be ranked in the order they finish. Number five: The bottom ten teams for a challenge may be eliminated at the judges's discretion. Number six: There are no do-overs. Number seven: All standard prohibitions on combustibles and death-defying projects apply during this competition."

"Borrrring," Cherub grumbles.

I read faster. "Number eight: Disqualified and eliminated teams will report to Mrs. Jalil's office to complete a community service project. It will be extremely rewarding and fun. Number nine: Once teams are confirmed at the end of Monday's homeroom, they may not be changed for any reason. Number ten: Teams who voluntarily withdraw from the competition will participate in the community service project with Mrs. Jalil."

When the read-aloud torment is finally over, Mr. Happy plops stacks of what look like business cards on the first desk in each row. "These are STEAMS competition punch cards. Take one and pass the rest back," he explains. "Each time you complete a challenge successfully, we'll mark your card so you can move forward."

Huey and I get our cards at the same time. They're shiny and about three times thicker than Huey's magic deck. STEAMS! is printed on the front in heavy black letters.

S   T   E   A   M   S   !

"A number between one and fifty-one is stamped on the back," Mr. Happy says. "That is your randomly assigned team."

I flip my card over. My number is eighteen.

I show it to Huey. His face goes white. His number is forty-five.

"As Dr. Yee said during assembly, you'll be able to make a few changes." Mr. Happy has to shout. Kids have already started checking numbers with their friends. Somebody's crying. Covert, under-desk swapping has already begun.

"But we encourage you to remain in your randomly assigned groups . . ." Mr. Happy's voice trails off, "so you meet new people."

Based on the noise levels on either side of us, the sixth- and eighth-grade homeroom teachers just delivered the instructions to their classes as well. Mr. Happy gets a text. A second later, the accordion doors slide back and all of middle school is together.

Mr. Happy and Ms. Latrice, the sixth-grade home-room teacher, look at each other helplessly. Fortunately for them, Coach Judy is in charge of eighth grade.

TWEEEEP!!

Everybody zips. Everybody sits.

"Mr. Happy, Ms. Latrice, and I are going to step out for exactly fifteen minutes," Coach Judy says. "During that time, you may swap cards with other students if you choose. Remember: Each team must have five students. And each team must have at least one student from each grade. Am I understood?"

Everybody nods.

TWEEEEP!! "Voices, please."

We speak: "Understood."

Coach Judy motions Ms. Latrice and Mr. Happy to the exit. We stay seated. We stay zipped. Until the door closes. Then our combined homeroom turns into *Game of Thrones.*

No matter what Dr. Yee and the teachers hoped would happen, kids be kids. Desks get pushed around. Chairs fall over. Everybody's shouting. Somebody's knee buzzes my ear. Somebody else uses a backpack to slide across the floor.

I weave through the crowd searching for spare sport-sters. For the record, this is one of those times when having more friends would be helpful.

Missy-Bella and Titus make a face at Ritchie then trample my right foot and dash away to form their own team. LaVontay head-butts my shoulder when Farrow plucks him out of the air while he's doing a fancy ballet move to get a group of eighth-grade arts peeps' to notice him.

Ritchie looks like somebody shoved a plate of brussels sprouts under his nose. "Dude! What are you doing? We said we were going to be 100% pure sportsters. Real sportsters play ball, hockey, lacrosse and stuff. They don't do"—he spits out the word—"ballet."

Farrow rolls his eyes. "Get real. Have you ever watched LaVontay practice? He's not just an arts peep. He's an athlete, man." He scans the room looking for another catch.

"Farrow! I'm over here!" Liam waves to get his attention. Farrow ignores him. He smashes my foot sprinting after JoJo Davies, a sixth-grade mathatron who also runs track.

It's too dangerous on the ground. I hop on a chair and scan the room. From up here, kids look like chess pieces. From the way they're waving at me, a bunch of those chess pieces want me on their team. If I do the right series of switches, I could definitely be on a team that's a contender for the top group.

"Pssst!" Thyme's twin sister, Winnie, jabs my shin with a pencil.

"Ow!"

She jabs me again. "Quiet!"

I hop off my chair to get my legs out of pencil range. "What?"

"You're in luck," Winnie hisses. "We're building a super team of technovengers. We've got space for two more." She crinkles her nose like a cat stalking a mouse. "You've got skills, Doug. You're an out-of-the-box thinker. I convinced the team to take you. Let's go."

I glance at Huey. Winnie follows my gaze. She shakes her head. "Nope. Just you."

"But . . ."

"Huey's okay in tech, but he freezes up sometimes. We need nerves of chromium to win." She leans in close. I suddenly realize she hasn't blinked once during this entire conversation. "Listen." Her voice drops to a whisper. "You're not the only one who wants to go to GadgetCon. And I know for a fact that Dr. Yee's going to pick somebody from the winning STEAMS team."

I must look skeptical. Winnie's intel isn't always reliable.

"It's true!" She yanks out her phone and jams it against my nose. I get a quick peek at a tiny, convoluted map that looks like the footprints of a dozen dancing spiders, before my eyes cross and my vision goes blurry.

"Too close!" I push her hand away. "That's giving me a headache."

"Just trust me then," Winnie snaps. "I heard it from Thyme, who got it from Angela, who heard it from Billy, who got a text from Mark, who says he overheard Dr. Yee telling Mrs. Jalil how he was going to pick who goes to GadgetCon. Can't argue with the facts." She smirks. "Join our team if you want to win, Doug."

Five minutes—and a bunch more recruiting pitches from other teams—later, I decide to look for Huey so we can strategize.

I finally spot him hopscotching through the crowd like a vampire hunter on a mission. He bargains and swaps and trades until he scores a punch card with the number eighteen. Then he dashes back, slams an arm across my shoulders, and hollers, "Package deal!" every time anybody comes close.

After a while, nobody does.

CHAPTER 5

T. W. Jackson-Zezzmer

Worst. Day. Ever.

I've been at school for more than two hours, and it's barely 10:00 A.M. I'm too cool for this, yo. Everyone says so.

Instagram says school's a waste because I'm a natural at football. Elliott says I'm a better player than he was at my age. He says I have quick feet and excellent hands. He doesn't stress about my future because I have focus, discipline, and grit.

It doesn't matter if my grades aren't shiny like Mr. Big Brain's. Ever since my last touchdown pushed Northeast Den to victory over City, everybody sees my potential. Everybody knows I'm the man.

"Are you with us, Terrell?"

Make that *almost* everybody. My English teacher, Ms. Hamilton, clearly didn't get the email.

I must have been daydreaming in class again 'cause I never heard her stop lecturing. But she did. Obviously. Now she's standing at the front of the room, fists on hips, giving me the evil eye. Thanks to her, everyone else is staring at me too. It's cool if they check me when I'm on the field. I don't like people watching me in school though.

I paste a look on my face that's supposed to say, "Spending an entire period discussing Shakespeare is fascinating, Ms. Hamilton. Of course I'm interested in stuff that's four hundred years old."

She glares harder. Which means my expression probably said, "Ms. H., your lecture's so boring, my brain cells passed out."

A moment later, the bell rings and Ms. Hamilton says, "Don't forget, your reports are due by Friday. Remember, this is a critical essay. Be thoughtful about what you write. I expect a profound evaluation of Shakespeare's works from each of you. As always, you should send your assignment to me by email. And one more thing"—she makes a point of looking at me—"this is a significant grade. If you fail, you'll have to retake my class in the summer."

That's not happening. At least not to me. I'm supposed to be the star of Elite Juniors this year. Ma's not as into sports as she used to be, but she got really excited about organizing a cheerleading squad for the moms. And I already know how Elliott will react if I miss the exhibition games because I'm stuck in summer school. He'll lose it. He's got his mind set on "both his boys"—me and Mr. Big Brain—following him into pro sports. He tells me that every night.

"You're a Zezzmer now, T.W. Sports are our family legacy."

"I'm relying on you to help Doug get excited about sports, T.W."

"I grew up in the poorest town in South Carolina, T.W. Sports were my ticket to the life we enjoy now. You and Doug have it easier than I did, but sports are your tickets to great lives too."

I like having a dad, but being a Zezzmer is a lot of pressure.

I dodge by Ms. Hamilton and dash out fast.

Free period's next. Ms. Hamilton doesn't allow electronics in her classroom, so I grab my laptop and phone from my locker, cram the paperback I brought from my stash at home in my pocket, and book toward my special spot under the stairs. Even Mr. Roosevelt, the custodian, doesn't go there during the day.

"J-Z!" My guidance counselor, Mr. Arbor, stands in his office door. He's one of those dudes whose name fits him exactly. Arbor = tree. Stick some leaves in his dreads, and he could double as a sequoia.

Back in the day, before Elliott and Ma got married, I did this thing. Spot a dude who kind of looks like me. Wonder if he's my dad. But no way with Mr. Arbor, even though that wouldn't be awful. His skin's as dark as midnight. Me and Ma's is more like the sun.

"I thought you and I should have a conversation before I call your parents with an update," Mr. Arbor says.

Everybody else in the world calls me T.W. or Terrell or Terrell Wallace if I'm really in trouble. Not Mr. Arbor. He uses the initials of my last name because . . . who knows. Adults call you what they want, no matter what you say.

I trudge into his office and sag into my usual spot. I'm here so much the creaky yellow chair with the ratty pleather cushion should be retired when I'm gone. It's a perfect fit most of the time, but this is the Worst Day Ever. So I'm sitting on the spine of one of my favorite books and even my usual chair's a pain.

Mr. Arbor leans on the edge of his desk and watches me squirm. "You need a plan for Ms. Hamilton's paper. Have you even started?" He sighs when I don't answer. Then he sticks out a hand. "I saw a book stuffed in your pocket when you walked in. Should I bet it isn't *The Tragedies of William Shakespeare*?"

"Noooo." I tug out the book. It's an ancient copy of *Foundation* by Isaac Asimov. I've read it a dozen times. The cover's torn, and my favorite pages are creased. I drop it in his hand.

"For someone who supposedly doesn't like to read, you sure read a lot of what you like," Mr. Arbor says.

"Umph." I roll my eyes. We've talked about how I got into sci-fi, when it was just me and Ma, living in a tiny apartment over a 7-11. Mr. Arbor knows why I like books about exploring different worlds, changing the future, stuff like that.

"There's nothing wrong with reading for fun," Mr. Arbor continues. "In fact, I encourage it. But as long as you're in this school, you have to read what's assigned as well. And you have to turn in your papers."

"Umph." I dig the heel of my shoe in the carpet.

Mr. Arbor stares at me. I look at the floor. Mr. Arbor keeps staring. So do I . . . until I can't anymore.

"It's not my fault!"

We've had this talk a dozen times.

Nobody knows why school papers are hard for me. Elliott paid for a bunch of tests after I became a Zezzmer. Whatever's going on in my brain isn't medical. It's some kind of block. I don't even bother trying to explain it anymore. All I know is that when I try to write for classes, the words I need get turned round and round like a blind-folded running back. They never make it out of my head and onto the paper the way they should. It's embarrassing, especially now that I have a stepbrother like Mr. Big Brain. He can write papers in his sleep.

"You figured it out earlier this year," Mr. Arbor says. "Your take-home exam about *The Three Musketeers* got an A."

"Umph." He would really be disappointed if he knew how that happened.

We go back to staring. This time Mr. Arbor breaks first. "I know you're not a fan of the classes we offer here. I'm the first to admit there isn't much choice—particularly for somebody who may want to write science fiction one day." He folds his hands and leans across the desk. His face collapses into one of the mushy sympathetic expressions he probably learned in public school guidance counselor class. "Have you talked with your parents yet about switching schools, J.Z.?"

"Noooo." I'm not looking forward to that conversation. Elliott convinced Ma that Northeast Den is the best school for me before we even moved here. Like he always says . . .

"There's a reason Northeast students always get picked for the top high school club teams, T.W. Northeast puts their money where their mouth is when it comes to sports."

"Being a starter on the right club team will get you a college scholarship, T.W."

"Once you show what you can do in college, you're headed for the pros."

Mr. Arbor is still talking. "Listen J-Z, I almost fell over the first time you said you wanted to go to Benjamin Banneker. Their sports teams aren't nearly as strong as ours, and until we started meeting regularly, I thought sports were your only passion. Now I know better. Maybe if you told your parents what you like about Banneker . . ."

"Umph." Why do adults insist on trying to get you to talk about things that you obviously don't want to talk about? Waste. Of. Time.

Elliott's already mad that Mr. Big Brain's mom won't switch him to Northeast when he starts high school. No telling what he'd do if he found out I check Benjamin Banneker's website every day to reread the course catalog, because—surprise!—Banneker's high school has a bunch of science fiction electives in the English department. It has an extra credit program called *Turn Science Fiction into Science Fact with STEM*. It has a library with thousands of books, and I'm pretty sure a bunch of them are sci-fi. And even though its sports teams aren't nearly as good as Northeast's, contrary to what Elliott says a lot of Banneker kids still get on top club teams too. Who *wouldn't* want to go to school there?

So far, Ma's on Elliott's side about Northeast. Probably because Grandma's always calling from Michigan and telling her not to rock the boat. Ma's not a pushover though. She always says I need a solid backup career plan since most college football players never make the pros. And what's more solid than being a sci-fi writer? I figure she'll back me on leaving Northeast if I ace sports camp, impress the college scouts and club team coaches, earn a spot on a top club team, and make Elliott proud, *before* I spring the news that I've been accepted at Banneker.

I'm on top of the sports thing. And I've been working on Banneker's entrance application for months. I've read the directions so many times, I can see them in my head.

1. Create an account. **Done!**
2. Complete an application. **Did that too!**
3. Students: Upload an essay about a subject that interests you. (Note, completing this step will automatically forward your materials to Assistant Principal Mrs. Jalil for evaluation.)
4. Parents and guardians: Complete the financial disclosure statement after you receive an acceptance letter from Mrs. Jalil.

Right now it's number 3 that's stopping me. Every time I try to write the essay, I don't know how to start. I feel like I'm trying to write a school paper.

It's impossible.

I can't do it.

Unless . . . What if I use the Shakespeare report for my essay? I can handle it the same way I did the *Three Musketeers* assignment. I get that it's straight-up cheating, but this will be the absolute last time.

Promise.

CHAPTER 6

Frederick Douglass Zezzmer

There's no way to sugarcoat it. STEAMS team selection was a horror show-catastrophe-disaster.

Sure, some kids lucked out. Their teams are perfect: 100% mathatrons, 100% sportsters, 100% science heads, yada, yada, yada. They're set if there are timed competitions. They won't have to waste time arguing because everybody on their teams thinks the same way.

The rest of us don't get everybody we want, so we're bummed. But even if all the bummed kids were put in a room together, nobody's as bad off as me. Thanks to Huey's package deal, I'm on the worst team possible: Me, Huey, Liam, The Shark, and Padgett Babineaux. We're the Island of Misfit Toys of STEAMS teams.

To make things worse, our first challenge isn't even about STEAMS. It's about building rapport or whatever. To get us started, we're supposed to create a name that says something meaningful about our group, then upload it to MeU by ten tonight.

"Check that box," Ritchie says, loud enough so everyone in the lunch line hears him. "Our team's already got a name. We're TheExcellentorators! We finished so fast we had time to write a song."

He group-grunts with LaVontay, Pixie, and JoJo. Then Farrow waves his arms like a conductor while the others TheExcellentorators sing.

> *Ex-cel-lent.*
> *Ex-cel-lent.*
> *Ex-cel-len-tor-a-tors.*
> *We're supersmart.*
> *We're also strong.*
> *We're genius alligators.*

"Not bad," The Shark says.

"It's actually pretty good," Padgett agrees. "Kind of catchy."

"It's amazing," Liam says. "That's why Farrow's the sportster king."

I can't believe my team. "What are you doing? You're not supposed to cheer the competition."

The Shark frowns. She's still carrying her backpack. Books bulge through the gaps. It's so heavy, she's half hunched over. For some reason she has a mechanical pencil stashed behind each ear. "You're not the boss of me," she says moodily.

"Well . . ." We haven't selected a leader yet. But if we want any shot at winning, it has to be me. "Your hair's crooked," I counter. She's got a new style today. Her dreads are coiled into Princess Leia buns. They're still lopsided, though.

"Don't antagonize her," Huey warns. "Look at all that stuff she's carrying. I heard she can bench press-three hundred pounds."

The Shark rolls her eyes up and to the side, kind of like I do when Moms or Julius asks me something I don't want to answer. She glares at me like a cranky goldfish.

"Shows what you know. My hair's supposed to be this way. I'm an astronaut-in-training. I'm doing a gravity experiment. Besides, astronauts-in-training have more important things to worry about than being stylish," The Shark sniffs. "And you shouldn't listen to rumors. They're always wrong. I can't bench-press three hundred pounds. Not yet anyway. But my dad says I'm freakishly strong for my size, so watch out." She wags a finger at us. "I'm going to win this competition. You two better not get in my way."

I am NOT scared of a sixth grader! But I heard she bit somebody one time. That's why everybody calls her The Shark. I take a step back just in case.

Unfortunately, I can't move too far. The food line for lunch is extra-slow. Which means two things:

First, even though we don't have classes this week, somebody's parents still showed up for Stump 'Em B4 You Lunch 'Em. It's one of the most popular sign-ups for B-B's parents' association. Parents lob questions at us before they hand over our lunch plates to burn off competitive energy before afternoon classes. A ticker by the counter keeps a running score.

And second, kids who got here early scarfed their food and are already back for seconds. So it can only be . . .

"Lasagna," Huey breathes. His stomach rumbles.

He's right. The serving stations are packed with huge pans of thick slabs of noodles shellacked together with sautéed vegetables and three different kinds of gooey cheese. There's a beef version for the carnivores; a turkey version for the poultritarians or whatever; a veggie version; a vegan version; a gluten-free version; and even a dairy-free version for the lactose intolerant. My mouth starts watering. I want one of each.

"Word to the wise," Ramón whispers as he hops into line for another serving, "my parents are lunch-duty volunteering today. They're quizzing on the periodic table."

Lucky for me, I memorized the periodic table in third grade while I was grounded for testing DougieZ's Clear as Glass Floor Wax & Indoor Ice Rink without warning Moms and Julius first.

"No prob," I say, puffing out my chest.

A shocked-looking eighth grader stumbles by clutching her dessert. *Score! It's lemon chocolate–chip pie!* She glares at Ramón. "Gaelic. I did not see that coming. You didn't tell me your parents spoke Gaelic, dude!"

Ramón's ears flame pink. "Sorry. You know how competitive parents get at Stump 'Em. My folks are kind of overachievers."

I slide my tray along the rails to the pickup spot. The ticker says, *Students: 60, Parents: 56.* The score is close, but parents are not getting a point on my watch.

"Guten Tag, Douglass," Ramón's dad says. "Extra Fleisch und extra Käse für dich heute, nehme ich an."

This is not Gaelic. I lucked out though. Ramón's dad can't help himself. He always gives little hints.

His eyes drift slightly to the left, toward the gigantic steaming wedges of extra-meat, extra-cheese lasagna that are obviously the top choice today. The pan is three-quarters empty. Even though I don't speak much, uh, German, it's easy to guess what Mr. Chavez said.

I nod at a hefty chunk of lasagna enthusiastically. "Yep. Load me up, please!"

Mr. Chavez looks relieved that I got it right. But rules are rules. He holds the plate a few inches above my tray before hitting me with his test. This one must be about the periodic table.

"Und die Frage: Was ist der Schmelzpunkt von Iridium?" His gaze flits to the melting cheese on my hunk of lasagna.

Melting. That's the giveaway! Elements on the periodic table have melting points and boiling points. Cheese isn't an element, but iridium—the only word I recognized in that tsunami of German—sure is. There's no way I can count to 2,466 in German, but . . . workaround!

"Zwei." I hold up two fingers.

"Vier." Four fingers.

"Sechs." Six fingers.

"Sechs." Six fingers.

"Celsius oder Fahrenheit?" Ramón's dad asks.

Easy one. "Celsius," I answer confidently.

Ramón's dad grins. He fakes a mic drop then slides my plate onto my tray and updates the ticker. *Students: 61, Parents: 56.*

Huey creeps into place behind me. "Hi, Mr. and Dr. Chavez." His voice quivers.

Ramón's mom smiles sweetly. "Hubert! Ungependa chakula gani cha mchana leo?"

"Swahili *and* the boiling point of gadolinium? Seriously? I should get bonus points for that," Huey grumbles when he finishes Stump 'Em. His hands are still shaking.

We scan the cafeteria looking for a good table.

STEAMS has ruined the regular seating structure. Before today, everybody had a favorite table. The popular kids even had special chairs. My and Huey's table was closest to the exit so we could scarf down food until the very last second.

But before we left homeroom, Coach Judy said we should eat lunch with our teams. She didn't give us tip sheets or anything. Nobody knows the appropriate seating protocol. Do we all sit down at the same time? Do we start eating together? Do we bow like in *The Lion King* and present our chocolate milk as an offering to our group's top kid?

Huey and I finally find a table that will fit our entire team. For the record, it's not even close to our regular place. We are at the most horrible location possible: a round table smack in the middle of the room.

Huey grabs the chair next to me while the rest of our group walks over. "Choosing teams was so weird. Everybody was buzzing around and stuff." He covers his mouth so no one else can hear him. "How come you chose these guys, Doug? A bunch of other kids wanted us. I heard them ask you while I was swapping cards. Being in some of those groups would've been awesome. But I figure you've got a plan. You've got a plan, right?"

I don't have the heart to tell him that his package deal requirement blew up any possible ideas. So I just grunt.

"Oh. Okay. Got it." Huey totally misreads the situation. He punches my arm. "Don't worry about it. Everybody messes up sometimes."

It takes two helpings of lasagna, three slices of dessert, the entire lunch period, plus the rest of the afternoon to come up with the saddest name of all time: TravLiUey-PadgeyZezz. As in Travis, Liam, Huey, Padgett, and Zezzmer.

We couldn't agree on anything else.

The Shark rejected TheZezzmerites, which, in my opinion, totally sings. I squashed her idea, Astronaut-in-Training & Others, because it was awful.

Liam couldn't come up with one decent sportster concept. Turns out he's still searching for his sports sweet spot, which is why he hauls a duffel full of "just in case" athletic equipment all the time. For the record, Liam's being a nonsportster sportster is probably why Farrow didn't want him in his group. Anyway, Liam thought we should call ourselves TheAthletiCats because, wait for it . . . he's secretly obsessed with being a cat veterinarian.

Huey was fine with anything I liked. And Padgett Babineaux didn't have any suggestions at all. None. Which makes no sense. She's Padgett Babineaux!

I heard she was banned from having a phone until she graduates from high school . . . because she used her last one to change Dr. Yee's opening slide during an important presentation. She switched up the school values. Respect, Kindness, Wisdom, Community, and Heart became Chew Gum, Longer Lunches, More Three-Day Weekends, Harder Tests, and Global Travel.

Epic! Where's that Babineaux creativity when we need it?

CHAPTER 7

Padgett Babineaux

From: babineauxp
To: grams

Hi Grammy,

This is your 1:00 P.M. reminder to take your afternoon blood pressure pill. Did you take it already? I hope so.

Please charge the B-B hot spot so we have Wi-Fi tonight. I told Mrs. Jalil the battery keeps going out. She said it's because we've had the hot spot on loan for two years already. It's old. She promised to get a new one for us soon. She's also checking on getting a phone for me so I can text you instead of sending emails when I'm at school. That's cool.

Guess what? We're having a special contest this week. It's called STEAMS. Did you read the email about it from Dr. Yee? He sent it last Friday. Maybe you forgot to tell me?

I'm on a team with two seventh graders (Doug and Huey), another eighth grader (Liam), and a sixth grader (real name Travis but kids call her The Shark. She's the one whose mother died of COVID. Remember? Mrs. Jalil put a message about her in an email.)

Most kids went w-i-l-d making teams. I didn't. I waited until Coach Judy had us call out the numbers on the back of our punch cards, then I went over and met my group. Boy, were they surprised. Doug usually talks a lot, but when he saw me, he didn't know what to say.

Our first assignment is to make a name for our group. Dr. Yee says what we call ourselves and what we call each other is important, so the names have to be special. Our name is TravLiUeyPadgeyZezz. It's just okay.

Doug wants us to have an anthem because this other group, TheExcellentorators, has one.

We may do a Zoom if we don't come up with a song this afternoon. That's why I need to be sure we have Wi-Fi.

We were supposed to share phone numbers so we could talk more. I told my group that I don't have a phone—but I didn't tell them why.

Oh, and another thing happened, too. It's raining! Have you looked outside? Even if you haven't, I bet you could tell. Guests are always extra messy when it's raining.

Hope it doesn't mean you have to work too hard. Mrs. Jalil said she'll drive me home because of the weather, so you don't have to leave early.

See you soon!

P.

CHAPTER 8

Frederick Douglass Zezzmer

The first day of STEAMS can't be over fast enough.
Spending an entire day with random kids I barely know is not what I go to school for. All that blah, blah, yammer, yammer, yap, yap small talk is stressful. How do grown-ups dream this stuff up?

On top of the agony of an afternoon of forced socializing, the bitter memory of TravLiUeyPadgeyZezz's reaction to my suggestion for a team song still burns. I used the DougApp to create the perfect tune. Then I put some serious effort into writing lyrics. They were amazing.

> *Who's the win, win, winningest team*
> *The judges will sezzz?*
> *It's me.*
> *It's us.*

It's Trav-Li-Uey-Padgey-Zezz!
Yaaaaaaay, team!

The critics were merciless. The Shark bared her teeth. "I'm not singing that. It's terrible."

Padgett agreed. "I'm not feeling it." She flicked her retainer and stomped off.

Liam wasn't helpful either. "Sorry, Doug. It kind of stinks."

Even Huey sold me out. "Not to throw shade or anything, but they're right. That song could use some work."

Between hating on my song, arguing for half an hour about whether to go to the library or an empty classroom to work after lunch, and not appointing me team leader even after I major-hinted twice, spending so much time with my so-called team was devastating. It's good we decided to cancel the Zoom call after we scrapped the song. The Trav-LiUeyPadgeyZezz crew is sucking out all my life force.

My phone buzzes while I'm walking to the middle school pickup lane with Huey. I check the caller ID before answering. It's T.W. *Great.* Today's misery just keeps coming.

"Hello."

"I have another paper." T.W. growls. He sounds the way a poked bear would sound if poked bears talked, instead of ripping your arms off and eating your head.

"So."

Huey gives me a puzzled look. I mouth, "T.W." Huey flinches and jogs ahead to the pick-up lane.

"So?" T.W. cuts back. "So, I don't have time to write it myself."

It would be great if he *asked* for help. I wouldn't be mean about it. At least, I don't think I'd be. I help people in B-B's peer tutoring program all the time. That's where I met Huey. And I volunteer for Literacy Is Lit Bookstore's homework helpline whenever I can. I have a five-star rating! I make schoolwork fun.

"Do what you do, Mr. Big Brain," T.W. grumbles.

"But . . ."

"Just play the game when Elliott calls. This'll be the last time." He hacks out something else before clicking off. If I didn't know better, I'd think it was "Thanks." But this is T.W., so hard nope on that.

I shove my phone back in my pocket. I'm only a few feet away from the pickup lane but the walk has never seemed so long. I slump next to Huey on the waiting bench.

"Want to see a card trick?"

I shake my head. "It won't help. T.W. wants me to write another paper." Huey's the only person I told about helping T.W. cheat on his *Three Musketeers* report. It happened almost two months ago, and I still feel terrible. Worse than that time I ate too much cotton candy at Disneyland. And I was sick for days.

"No way! You can't do that again." Huey's eyes go wide. He's seen Moms angry. It's not something he'll ever forget. "If your mom finds out, you're done for, man. Her hair will literally catch on fire. Then she'll ground you until you leave for college."

He's right. And it's not just Moms. She and Julius are on the same page about cheating. They don't double-team punish me that often, but when they do, it's not fun.

I muster up my courage. "So what if T.W. does put Super Glue in my toothpaste? I'm not helping him cheat again. I'm done." Saying that out loud was easier than I thought. Then again, it was just for practice.

"Good choice." Huey looks proud. "I think I was wrong about your folks grounding you until college. That would be too easy. They won't let you out of your room until you're thirty. You'll be ancient."

My phone buzzes again. This time I'm ready for T.W. But it's a text from Pops instead.

Pops: How was your day, son? That early morning walk got your blood flowing, didn't it?

I flex my fingers. Luckily, my hands thawed out way before this call.

Me: Blood flowing. Yep.

Pops: And it was fun, right?

If I don't turn this conversation around, we're going to have another one of those angry talks where words slam together like bumper cars. I suck in a breath and ignore Pops's question.

Me: About school, Pops. Did you see the email about the special contest we're having? The winning team gets a trophy.

Pops: 💬

Huey leans in and peers at my phone. "What's going on?"

Pops: A trophy? That's fantastic! I'm glad that school of yours is coming around. What's the trophy for? Football? Baseball? Field hockey? Hoops? I can help.

Oh man.

Me: Thanks Pops. There'll be some sports, but it's probably mostly a STEM and arts competition. That's still good, right? I heard Dr. Yee will choose who goes to GadgetCon from the winning team!

Pops: 💬

I type faster.

Me: The Elders say it's important for people to decide what they like then follow their passion. They have lots of examples. Like, did you know Dr. Myron Rolle was in the NFL before he became a neurosurgeon?

Pops: 💬

"Why's it taking him so long to text back?" Huey asks.

I twist my neck until it cracks. "He goes to Greg G.'s website to double-check almost everything. Plus, he still uses all of his fingers to type. That takes forever."

Huey taps my phone screen. "Check it out. He wants to help."

"Only because sports are involved. Sports are part of his plan to turn me into an EZ Clone, remember? He only cares about the stuff he's good at. That's why he's not interested in inventing."

Pops: You quote the Elders a lot, son. I think those barbershop classes might be becoming a distraction. You spend too much time there. The research says children perform best when they're focused. I think you should quit those classes. I'll talk with your mother.

I grip the phone tighter. My gut starts to clench. It's not just Pops dissing the Elders' Culture & History lessons that bothers me. Julius and I have been going to monthly classes at the barbershop, followed by lunch at

Miss Margeaux's Diner, since I was four. It's our man time. I won't give that up.

Pops: One more thing. T.W. needs help with English. That's why we had a conference this morning. He's got a big paper on Shakespeare due on Friday. If he doesn't pass, he'll have to do summer school instead of sports camp. We can't have that. You did a great job helping him a few months ago. I need you to do that again.

He's not asking. I bet he's doing the EZ stare.

Me: But Pops . . .

Pops: He'll email his assignment to you so you can look it over. I'll clear it with your mother.

And he's not listening. How are we ever supposed to learn to compromise if he won't listen? Moms says we're a lot alike sometimes. I don't see it. Not. At. All.

Pops: T.W. needs that paper turned in pronto. It can't be late. Handle it today or tomorrow, okay?

Pops might give me a break from writing the paper if I tell him about the cheating, but then he'd be so mad there's no way he'd agree to let me go to GadgetCon even after Dr. Yee chooses me.

I have to win STEAMS, write T.W.'s stupid paper, and keep my mouth closed about the cheating. What choice do I have?

Me: Okay.

Pops: Great. I knew I could count on you.

CHAPTER 9

Frederick Douglass Zezzmer

Huey's already left with his first stepdad when our ancient Subaru pulls into the pickup lane. Julius is driving. His R&S Corporate Accounting work ID ("Hello! I'm Julius Jordan, senior accountant") dangles from a lanyard looped around the rearview.

Moms waves from the passenger seat. It's weird that she's here today. She usually works late on Mondays. She couldn't have found out about the cheating—or could she? Moms's Spidey sense is ridiculous if she's not distracted. *Aw man.* I start chewing the inside of my cheek. I lean in for a closer look. Her hair's not on fire. My secret's still safe. Something's up, though.

Moms gives me an up-and-down squint, like she always does when she sees me for the first time after I spend a few nights with Pops. She doesn't say anything bad, though. She can't. The first few weeks after Pops came back were so rough that she and Pops went to a mediator. Now they're doing this program called Conscious Compassionate Co-Parenting, because the mediator said Pops should ease into being a hands-on father. CCCP means (1) nobody says anything bad about anybody else in front of the kids, and (2) original parents rule. That's Moms and Pops in my case; Patrice and . . . nobody, I guess . . . for T.W.

CCCP doesn't regulate looks, though. Moms's skin is dark brown like mine, but I can still see her cheeks flush. If that's not enough of a giveaway, I watch as she wrinkles her nose and blinks.

Wrinkle-blink 1–4 means, *What the heck's going on with his hair?*

Wrinkle-blink 5 means, *And what's the deal with those clothes?*

Wrinkle-blink 6–10 means, *And did they really let him out of the house in those holey shoes? I swear, I'm calling Elliott after Doug goes to bed and we're having a serious talk.*

CCCP also means that Julius is stuck on the sidelines, which is why I think it sucks. My folks aren't big fans either. The night they told me about it, Julius looked like somebody puked on his winning lottery ticket. "I wish we had another option, too," he admitted. "But it's what the mediator recommended and it's supposed to work well. Besides, I agree with your mom. It's really important to try this. It may help you and Elliott re-bond."

Moms says CCCP won't last much longer. She only agreed to try it until June.

Pops wants us to keep doing it forever. He says it's because Greg G. likes the program. I think it's because he gets jealous when I want to spend time with Julius, and CCCP gives him an edge. But whenever Pops acts like Julius doesn't matter, I feel like that model volcano I made in third-grade science. I just want to blow.

CCCP isn't the problem today, though. Car rules say that the first question when I get in the car is: "How was your day?" Yeah well, that was before STEAMS. I don't wait for Moms and Julius to ask.

"Today was the worst day ever." I vomit details about everything except T.W.'s paper. "I've got the worst team. I hate STEAMS. I've got the worst team. The name we came up with is stupid. I've got the worst team. We don't have an anthem. And . . . did I mention? I've got the worst team."

Julius eyeballs me in the rearview. "But how do you feel about your team?"

Moms cough-giggles before I can choke out a comeback. I can't help it. After a minute, I laugh a little, too.

Before Julius pulls away from the curb, he taps a button on the Subaru's dashboard. It's Zezzmer's Auto Proofer, one of my inventions. The button activates tiny cameras I placed by the brake lights, front lights, taillights, turn signals, and license plates. The cameras send time- and date-stamped photos to Julius's phone and email, and to the cloud. If he gets pulled over or has an accident, he'll have proof that everything was working the way it should. The Auto Proofer's only a prototype. It still has issues—like sometimes the little cameras fall off in the car wash, or they don't stop recording when the car's turned off, or they get too hot and scorch the paint—but Julius likes it anyway. He uses it every time he starts the car.

"I'm sorry STEAMS was awful today," Moms says. "Dr. Yee was very enthusiastic about it in his email. It sounds like a good idea to us parents. You're not giving up, are you?"

"No. I'm going to win. But it won't be easy. I have the worst team, Moms."

"Right." She taps the armrest between the driver and front passenger seats. Julius looks at her and smiles. "Well, there're two more bits of news to share," Moms says. "First, you and Julius are dropping me off at the airport. I have to fly to Seattle for some emergency meetings." She sighs. "I think it's another test to see who gets the promotion. It's going to take the entire week."

"Emergency meetings? Moms, you work for a company that makes baby clothes."

"(A) Infant attire is a highly competitive industry, and (B) I could be the next head of marketing for my firm. I have to go," Moms says primly. That explains why she's wearing her fancy threads and why her braids are pulled back in a "you need to take me seriously" bun. "The other news is that I talked with Huey's mother this afternoon. She and his dad and his stepparents need some alone time, so Huey's going to stay at our house for the rest of the week. You'll pick him up tomorrow morning on the way to school." I grunt and she swivels around to look at me. "I thought that would make you happy."

"It does, except . . ." I'm too bummed about all of the things that already went wrong with STEAMS to be happy, so all I say is, ". . . I have the worst team."

It stops raining by the time we say goodbye to Moms at the airport. There's even a rainbow covering our entire block when we get home. Julius still looks super-sad. After all these years as a family, he's used to Moms traveling, but he still gets sad when she goes out of town.

Our next-door neighbor, Mr. Cohen, is on his front porch doing deep knee bends and side twists. He's training for the Colorado Senior Games in July. He used to be a corporate attorney. Now, he helps me with trademark and patent applications for my inventions. His message T-shirt says *Happily Retired Since None of Your Beeswax*.

"Afternoon . . . Julius." Mr. Cohen puffs out a word each time a twist points his face in our direction. "Hi . . . F.D." He likes to use my initials. I don't know why. "Annie's . . . flight . . . take . . . off . . . okay?"

"It did, Nate. Thanks for asking," Julius calls as he trots to our door. "Are you joining us for dinner tonight? I'm making my famous *everything but the kitchen sink stew* to cheer up Doug."

Two things about Julius are legendary: his garden and his meals.

Everybody's speechless when they see the garden for the first time. It takes up half of our backyard. And there are even two raised planters in front of the house and miniature lemon and orange trees in the sunroom. He grows so much food that we were able to share fresh fruits and vegetables with our neighbors during the pandemic.

When it comes to cooking, Julius could probably be a world-class chef if he wanted to. He gets a kick out of coming up with weird names like *inside-out whatchamacallit burgers, D'oh! I forgot the eggs omelets,* and *spaghetti with maybe next time you'll clean the litter box meatballs.*

Everything but the kitchen sink stew is one of my favorites. It's packed with chunky homegrown vegetables ladled over extra spicy red, brown, and black rice. It's delicious.

Mr. Cohen thinks so, too. He stops exercising long enough to beam at us. "Regular time?"

Julius smiles back. "Regular time." He doesn't need to be specific. Mr. Cohen knows when dinner is served. He lived with us during the pandemic. It happened like this:

1. When lockdown started, Moms and Julius invited Mr. Cohen to stay in our spare room since his wife died a long time ago and he doesn't have relatives to check on him.
2. Mr. Cohen said, "I don't want to be a bother. I think I'll be fine. I can put a chair by the window. Maybe you could wave at me sometimes?"
3. Then Moms told us, "There's no way a seventy-year-old man is going to sit alone in that house month after month if we can help it."
4. Then Mr. Cohen learned the hard way that, unless she says it, Moms is allergic to the word no. I could've told him that if he'd asked me up-front. (For the record, I've seen Mr. Cohen smile a million times, but I've never, ever seen him grin as big as he did when he carried his special blanket, his special pillow, and the silver-framed picture of his wife into his new room.)

"I'll squeeze in a few bicep curls then pop over," Mr. Cohen says. "I baked some bread this morning. Want me to bring it with?"

Julius and I yell "Yes!" at the same time. Mr. Cohen's bread is the best.

After dinner (everybody), dishes (just me), and feeding our cat, Barack Opawsma (just me again), I head out to tinker in my workshop.

From the outside, my workshop looks like a toolshed, which is what it used to be. But on the inside, it's inventor heaven. Loops of wires hang from hooks by the window. A footlocker full of wheels, sprockets, metal plates, and computer guts sits by the door. A stack of tools rests on a table. A pile of broken machines that Julius and I scavenged during our last trip to Mr. Jake's Salvage Yard lies underneath.

Julius knocks on the door an hour after Mr. Cohen leaves for the evening.

"Time to talk?" His nails are caked with mud, which means he's been working in the garden. He likes to sift dirt and check plants' roots with his hands.

He juts his chin at the tangle of cables and washers sticking out of a dissected Roomba vacuum. "Is that Zezzmer's Solar-Powered Poop Scooper, or Doug's Remote-Controlled Cat-Walking Machine?"

"It's the cat walker. I'm trying to make it run quieter. So far, Barack Opawsma's not a fan."

"Uh-huh." Julius bumps around my workshop some more. He's about as subtle as a truck.

"You're wondering if the STEAMS competition is as bad as I think it is, aren't you?"

Julius fiddles with the cat walker's retractable leash. "It crossed my mind." He studies me. "But I also know your dad's very excited about Elite Juniors sports camp. He told your mom about it last weekend. He thinks it's a good opportunity for you two to spend more time together, and for you to meet some of his old friends from the Broncos and ESPN. He also says it will give you quality time with T.W. You haven't said much about it, though. Summer's only a few months away."

Minefield alert!

The last thing I want to do is spend more time with T.W. All we do together when Pops isn't around is watch football. But if I start complaining, Julius will ask a thousand questions. So, I ignore the sports camp comment and trot across my workshop to give him a fist bump. "It's all good."

And guess what? The minute I say those words out loud, I realize they're true. Even when people are skeptical about my inventions, they usually come around if I'm persistent. I laid the groundwork for being TravLi-UeyPadgeyZezz's leader today. By tomorrow, everybody will be on the same page.

CHAPTER 10

Travis Elizabeth Cod

I AM
an
astronaut–
in-training.

I WILL BE
the first person
to walk
on
Mars.

Daddy says,
"That's a big idea, Buttons.
But be careful.

Life can change
without warning."

In my head,
Mommy says,
"Big ideas are perfect
for you, Beetle-Bug."

In my head,
Mommy says,
"Once you know
what it is that you're wanting,
you need a
'how to get what you're wanting' plan."

So I wrote my plan
on sticky notes
and put them
in the closet
in my bedroom.

But I haven't even finished
Step 1
yet.

Because before I
can go to Mars,
I have to get into
Astronaut Camp . . .
in California.

It turns out,
getting into
Astronaut Camp
in California
is hard.

"So sorry," they say
every *time I send an application.*
"Your body's too small to be with the big kids.
Your brain's too big to be with the little kids.
The online tests say
you don't work well
in teams."

"So sorry," they say
every *time I send an application.*
"You don't fit in at this moment.
But keep smiling!
Maybe things will be better

for you
next time."

I hate it when grown-ups say,
"Keep smiling!"

I hate it when grown-ups say,
"Things will be better
next time."

It's like
waiting
in a
supermarket line
forever.

It's like sitting
in the backseat of a
too-hot
car.

It's being stuck
and doing nothing
and going nowhere
for infinity.

And I do not like
being stuck
anywhere,
for any amount
of time.

Which is why
I'm going to use
this stupid STEAMS competition
to prove that I do so
know how to
work in teams.

TravLiUeyPadgeyZezz
is going to win,
WIN,
W-I-N!
Even if I have to drag them
kicking and screaming
across
the final
finish
line.

CHAPTER 11

Frederick Douglass Zezzmer

I wake up happy and ready to take on the world. My brain is buzzing with ideas of how to lead TravLiUey-PadgeyZezz to victory.

First step: Check MeU for updates. Good call. Dr. Yee posted a letter to the entire middle school. He says he's bringing in special expert guest judges to watch us compete because STEAMS has "unconventional" challenges. We'll meet the judges in assembly.

Big deal. It doesn't matter how many judges there are. I only have to impress Dr. Yee. It'll be easy, right? Ugh. Wrong. Dr. Yee included a list of all fifty-one STEAMS team names in his post. IxnayOnTheBodySpray, StillCan'tOpenOurLockers😵, and We'llFixGlobal Warming are so creative. TheNeverLastonians is magic. TravLiUeyPadgeyZezz sticks out like a sore thumb.

"I'm sure your team will do just fine today, honey," Moms says during our morning FaceTime.

Julius is banging around in the kitchen. The aroma of *just 'cause they're blue doesn't mean they're blueberry pancakes* fills the air. He's already dressed for work. He's wearing a white shirt, blue tie, and black pants like always. He's so predictable. He can get ready in, like, five minutes. He's even faster than me—and I just grab whatever's not wrinkled and go.

I can tell Moms is distracted even through the screen. She's only put makeup on her eyebrows and eyes so far. The top of her face looks steely and ready for business. The rest of it is still regular. It'll take another twenty minutes of makeup, meditation, and chanting affirmations for her to switch from being Annie/Moms/Language Learner/Ceramics Maker/Julius's Favorite Garden Assistant to super serious corporate manager, Ann Zezzmer Jordan.

"Are you still excited about your meetings?" I ask.

Moms's mouth pinches into a makeup-free line. "The first meeting was fine, but then I had a conversation about the promotion that wasn't what I'd hoped for."

"How come?"

Moms blinks. I think she's trying to decide how much to tell me. I know the feeling.

Since her eyes are all made up, I get the full-on corporate, power woman stare. It's unnerving.

"There would be a lot more travel. More people to supervise. A great deal more work," she admits. "And the salary increase isn't as much as I expected based on what other people at that level are making." She sighs. "It's a hard decision."

"It doesn't sound hard to me. More work. Less money. Less fun. I vote no. Stay in your same job."

That gets a laugh. "I'll consider your advice, honey. But sometimes things aren't just black and white. There's a lot of gray to think about. We tapped into our emergency fund during the pandemic. And we're saving for your college fund. If I take the promotion, there's always a chance my salary will come up after I prove myself . . . again."

"Or you could move to another company. Fantastiske Babywear is always trying to hire you away." Julius eases my laptop across the table and slides a huge stack of pancakes under my nose. Then he puts a cup full of steaming hot maple syrup next to my plate. He melted a dollop of butter in the syrup just like I like it. I drench my pancakes and cram a huge forkful in my mouth. They're soooo good. I can't help but smile.

Moms licks her lips. "Those pancakes look amazing!"

My mouth is full so I give her a thumbs-up.

She laughs again. "I wish I could climb through this laptop and join you for breakfast."

"We do too," Julius says. He heads back to the stove to get his pancakes. "You know, you could also start your own marketing firm like we talked about," he calls over his shoulder. "Money will be a little tight at first, but I've got us. We'll be fine. And I'm pretty sure a lot of your current company's competitors will want to hire you on the spot."

Moms's forehead crinkles. "I've always wanted my own business." She's thinking hard. "Taking the leap would be scary. But . . . maybe I'm ready. Y'all think I'm ready?" She sounds like Huey. I guess even parents get a bad case of nerves sometimes.

"You're ready!" Julius calls.

I nod enthusiastically, but duck my head so she can't see my face. I pretend to chew. My pancakes taste like straw now.

I know it's selfish—and it probably would never happen—but I can't help worrying what might happen if money gets tight. Will there be less spare cash to buy the stuff I need for my workshop? Inventing materials can be pricey. I want Moms to be happy. But if we have to pinch pennies, Moms and Julius may ask me to swap inventing for the sports stuff Pops wants me to do. And even a little interruption would put a major dent in my prime inventing years.

I'm in a surly mood when Julius and I pile into the Subaru after breakfast, and head out to pick up Huey. Julius taps the Zezzmer's Auto Proofer and pulls out of the driveway. Mr. Espinoza waves to us from across the street before he hops into his Toyota. He's field-testing Zezzmer's Auto Proofer, too.

I must be radiating unhappy vibes because Julius checks me in the rearview when we hit the corner of Mary Bethune Drive and Monroe Street. It's kind of like he always does at intersections, but also kind of a little bit more.

When I don't say anything, he cranks up the volume on his favorite satellite channel, Da Broadway Boyz, blows out a breath, and eases into the crosswalk.

He's clearly planning to take Monroe to First Avenue, where Huey's mom and second stepfather live. Not a good choice. I did the research. Potholes. Workers fixing potholes. Spotters watching workers fix potholes. All on top of the regular traffic lights and four-way stops. I can't be late on the first day of STEAMS eliminations.

"Bethune's better."

Julius freezes. "What?"

And. Now. We're. Stopped. A lady walking her Frankendoodle cruises by us, and her dog keeps stopping to pee.

"Nothing." I spit the word out fast and loud then pop in my earbuds. I bob my head like I'm listening to killer beats.

Julius doesn't buy it. He narrows his eyes in his *I don't know what you're up to, but I know you're up to something* style.

I know I should let it go. Moms is always saying I need to ease up and let other people make decisions, which I totally would if they weren't always doing things wrong. I flip to Plan B major fast: Broadway singalong distraction. Julius loves to sing while he drives.

Problem is, I can't sing on key and I always mess up the lyrics. It doesn't matter what the song is. I never get the words right. The technical name for this is mondegreen. I learned about it on the internet. It's definitely a thing.

Julius is still eyeballing me, so I start hollering out his all-time fave from *The Lion King* and motion for him to sing along.

"FROM THE WAY WE DECIDE WHERE TO PLANT IT . . ."

Julius flinches.

"AND WIN KEYS STUCK UNDER A THUMB . . ."

Julius hits the gas. We lurch through the intersection and into the next block. But we're still on Monroe.

"Bethune." I can't help myself.

Julius sucks in a breath.

"Bethune would be faster."

Julius isn't a fan of backseat drivers. I can't tell for sure, but I think his neck veins may be throbbing. The hair at the top of his dad 'do starts to pulse.

"You need to turn right at Bethune then left at Aspen then left again at Cesar Chavez then go to First Avenue from there," I blurt. "I used DougApp to calculate the route. Going my way will save at least fifteen minutes."

Julius's ears twitch. I know what he's thinking: *Stick to my directions? Or listen to DougApp?*

DougApp wins. Like I said, Julius is predictable. He can't help himself here—he's a big-time blerd, just like me.

We take Bethune.

Thanks to DougApp's route, we're back on schedule when we get to Huey's house. His mom steps out on the porch to wave when we drive up. "Hi, Doug. Hi, Julius. Thanks so much for taking Huey. You're a lifesaver for helping on such short notice."

Huey suffers through a hug and a huge, sloppy kiss on the cheek from his mother, before he wriggles away. His fat blue duffel, the one he uses to schlep his stuff between his parents' houses or to my house when he's staying over, is half on the sidewalk and half in the street. When Julius pops the lock to the hatchback, Huey kicks his bag to the back of our car. He groans like he's dying when he hefts it inside.

"Need some help?" Julius asks.

"I got it, Mr. J." Which, for the record, is kind of true, but also kind of not. Huey's face is splotchy when he finally slams the trunk and collapses next to me in the backseat.

My mood gets a little better when Julius is back on the road. Huey and I do the long version of our secret shake. It's basically the short version done twice (one time forward, once in reverse), plus two ankle thwonks, and, the latest addition, the soon-to-be-famous Zezzmer-Linkmeyer Belch.

We've been perfecting our technique for weeks. It's megaloud. And potent! A cloud of vapor-stink moves from the backseat to the front in record time. In a flash, the car reeks with the smell of my half-digested pancakes and Huey's . . . I can't tell what exactly. He probably made it himself. I think whatever it was had applesauce, sardines, and pickles.

Julius gags. "Sweet Great-Grandmother Jones!" He pinches his nose with one hand and paws at his streaming eyes with the other.

"Hands on the wheel! Eyes on the road!" Huey and I bark.

"DougApp says that parents with two or more kids our age in the car are statistically 13.7 times more likely to be involved in preventable accidents because of distracted driving." I use my *you really should know better* voice. "You need to focus more, Julius."

Huey nods solemnly. "Word."

We fist-bump and finger-snap. Assuming we survive Julius's driving for the next three years, we're going to crush Drivers' Ed in high school.

There's only one entrance to Benjamin Banneker. That doesn't stop Julius from doing his usual paranoid-y, super-careful approach to the giant wooden double gates. All the parents drive like that. Spring is when the older tenth graders get their learner's permits and when eleventh graders can finally drive alone. Julius says navigating with new drivers on the road is like being stuck inside an old-fashioned Pac-Man game. He's not sure how he'll handle it when I start.

Except for the gates with the B-B logo and Benjamin Banneker quote carved deep in the wood, B-B doesn't look like a school from the outside. All sorts of trees—pine, fir, cottonwood, spruce, aspen, apple, peach, crabapple, cherry, and pear—line the tall, wrought-iron fence that marks the perimeter of the property. Between the trees and the fence, and the gates, nobody who's not allowed to be on campus can get in.

Each family gets a designated sensor for their car. When Julius gets close, the double gates swing open. The quote splits in two. The whole first sentence is on the left side. The second sentence is on the right.

Presumption should never	||	*Nor despair make us*
make us neglect that	||	*lose courage at*
which appears easy to us.	||	*the sight of difficulties.*

The sentences are formal and old-timey, but Benjamin Banneker's basically saying don't ignore the quick wins and don't give up when life gets hard.

Huh. The other team names had me worried about STEAMS again, no lie, but reading the quote today gives my brain a major reset. I'd give Benjamin Banneker a fist bump if he were here. Instead, I bow my head Wakanda-style at the gates.

Huey looks at me like I'm bonkers. His first stepdad taught him American Sign Language, and he taught me. *What are you doing?* he signs.

Getting ready to rumble, I sign back. *Let's go win STEAMS!*

CHAPTER 12

Huey Linkmeyer

Who changed the rules about where to sit in assembly? There's nothing on Me U!

Doug's all revved up, but I can tell assembly's going to be a disaster the second we walk in.

First off, Missy-Bella and her team sit in our seats in row JJ. They've got their feet on the backs of the chairs in front of them. They make it clear they're not going to move.

Second off, the rest of the auditorium is full of kids stumbling around like moths smacking into porch lights. They go to their regular section. Then they remember that yesterday Coach Judy said everybody should sit with their teams for the rest of the week. Then they have to find five empty seats that aren't too close to other kids they think are horrible. That's way harder than it sounds.

The whole thing is stressing me out!

And third off, TravLiUeyPadgeyZezz has to sit by the stage near a bunch of arts peeps teams because most of the other seats are taken when Padgett finally rolls in. She doesn't even apologize.

I wonder why she's late. She doesn't tell us why she's late. I bet she's late because she's in trouble. She walks in with Mrs. Jalil.

Most days, Dr. Yee and whoever does announcements stand during assembly. Today, Mr. Happy, Ms. Latrice, and Coach Judy help Dr. Yee drag four tall director chairs to the stage.

"Good morning, B-B middle schoolers!" Dr. Yee flashes the Vulcan hand salute. "Welcome to Day Two of Benjamin Banneker's inaugural STEAMS competition. Exciting, am I right?"

Somebody whoops.

"Thank you, Ramón! Everybody, give it up for Ramón!"

Somehow Ramón got snagged for Missy-Bella's team. He looks miserable. He barely lifts his head to answer, "Not me!"

Dr. Yee blazes on. "Your first challenge was to come up with a name that tells us something about your team. Before we review the results, I want to introduce our special guest judges. This is so coolio!"

Coolio? I think Dr. Yee sometimes forgets he's not a kid anymore. I wonder if I'll be like that.

After a minute, Dr. Yee realizes that saying coolio isn't that cool. He arches his eyebrows and snaps back to being a grown-up. "How many of you knew that UrBaniTeC Global Innovations recently moved its headquarters offices to Denver?"

Every hand shoots up. UrBaniTeC's inventions keep them in the news. Last month they introduced foldable, recyclable, temporary houses. The month before that they launched sneaker inserts that play music when you bounce.

"That's good to know," Dr. Yee says. "UrBaniTeC's founder and CEO was so excited about our STEAMS competition that she wanted to come here personally to participate. Give a warm B-B welcome to the brains behind UrBaniTeC Global Innovations. The holder of an amazing two hundred patents. UrBaniTeC's CEO, The DOM herself, Dr. Destiny Octavia Moore!"

"Check it out. She's in her power kicks!" Doug says, poking me. Sure enough, The DOM is wearing black, high-top sneakers just like she does for all of UrBaniTeC's important presentations.

Dr. Yee grins at her all goofy, like they're old-time friends. I feel embarrassed for him. Then, The DOM goofy-grins back.

"True fact: Dr. Yee and I met in middle school," she says. "We were . . ."

"Unique," Dr. Yee butts in. "I was the only Asian kid in our grade. Everyone expected me to be naturally good at science and math, which truth be told, I was not. I loved those subjects, but it took a lot of extra effort for me to do well in my classes."

"And I was the only Black girl in our entire school!" The DOM says. "Everyone expected me to be good at basketball, track, and choir, which"—she does what looks like a secret handshake with Dr. Yee—"truth be told, I was not!" It must be an inside joke. "I never made a basket in basketball, finished anything better than last place in track, or sang one note on-key through all of middle school. That's a long time to be bad at something. I enjoyed math and science though. I was good at them, too."

"Correction. She was amazing," Dr. Yee cracks. "She was my homework help buddy."

"We found each other in math club, which wasn't hard since we were the only two there. We've been best friends ever since," The DOM adds. "So when David, um, Dr. Yee, invited me to meet you, of course I said yes."

She beams at us. "Dr. Yee and two members of my senior team will judge STEAMS's preliminary elimination rounds today and tomorrow. I'll come back on Thursday to help select the winner. I understand you'll have a fun party all day on Friday to celebrate."

Two other grown-ups come out. The man is tall and bony. He's got a shaggy brown man-bun and a long, scruffy beard. The woman is even taller. Maybe because of her cowboy boots.

The DOM motions to man-bun man. "This is Mr. Montanari. He's our vice president of global product distribution. He decides which of our new ideas get sent to stores around the world."

"'ulloooo!" Mr. Montanari says. Large, square teeth peek through his beard. "'Ow'r ye, ye wee B-Bs? Guud idees ye gut, ain o' mur, yeh? Noh?"

"I guess I should have mentioned that Mr. Montanari's from Scotland." The DOM and Mr. Montanari fist-bump.

"And this is Dr. Campbell," The DOM says. She smiles at the woman like they're buds. "Every company needs someone to ensure products are safe and top quality before they launch. It's incredibly important work. Dr. Campbell has that role for UrBaniTeC."

"Howdy, kids," Dr. Campbell drawls. "Like The DOM said, my group and I make sure products are top-notch before they roll out the door. Fix them glitches so you don't need stitches, I always say."

She sounds like Grandpa! Doug rolls his eyes, but I like Dr. Campbell already.

"Word to the wise for y'all though," she continues. "I'm a tough judge. I'm going to put you through your paces. Make sure your work's up to snuff before I come around, ya hear?"

"And on that note, let's get this competition started!" Dr. Yee lowers the projection screen. He logs in to MeU. A second later, a three-column list of team names fills the screen.

AllTheElsas	ThisIsADumb-Challenge	TallerThanOur-Grandpas
Do-Re-We-Win	$A^2 + B^2 = BeatU$	EmbraceTheNerd
TheExcellentorators	WeScareOurselves-Sometimes	WeDreamAboutFlying
WeAllLikeGum-drops	TravLiUeyPadgey-Zezz	TheNeverLastonians
We♥Math	RMomsWillBeMad-IfWeLose	WeBelieveInYetis
Lil'Notes♪♪	TheTriangleLites	We'reGoodAtRiddles
MorePopQuizzes-Please	TheImprovAbles	WeStudyRocks
Do-OversRule	WeBeB-BChampions	Plié'sTheThing

TotallyUnstoppable

WhyAreWeDoing-
This?

NeverEverEver-
GiveUp

We'llFixGlobal-
Warming

IxnayOnTheBody-
Spray

FriendsSincePre-
school

GirlsRockScience

BladesOfGrassAre-
PeopleToo

WeDon'tKnowWhat-
ToCallOurselves

TheMightyCrafty-
Craftonizers

WeDoNOTLike-
EachOther!

VegansRTougher-
ThanUThink

Let'sDiscussThe-
DressCode

StillCan'tOpenOur-
Lockers😵

1OfUsLostAGerbil-
In2ndGrade

Waiting4Our-
GrowthSpurt

StraightThroughThe-
GoalPosts

WeBelieveInPrizes-
ForParticipation

SlightlySleepDeprived

Sportsters4Ever

NoGradingOnThe-
Curve

IsSTEAMS4AGrade?

AlwaysOnTimeFor-
Class!

MakerSpaceDemons

WeMayWimpOut

SoMatureWeShouldBe-
InHighSchool

PickingANameIsHard!

"Your first challenge was to create a team name that tells us something important about your group," Dr. Yee says. "Let's see how you did. Judges, which team should start?"

The DOM, Mr. Montanari, and Dr. Campbell whisper for a minute. "We'd like to hear from We♥Math," The DOM says.

Five girls hop up. "We chose We♥Math for our name because we're really good at math and we love how you can figure almost anything out with numbers. Nobody gets upset with math either. The answer's right or it's wrong," Bunny Silverstein says.

"Good call. Everybody, give it up for We♥Math!" Dr. Yee claps a few times, then moves on to the next team.

It goes like that for ten minutes. It's not nearly as bad as I thought. Nobody gets disqualified or anything.

When it's our turn, The Shark explains how we used parts of all of our names to create TravLiUeyPadgeyZezz so that everybody's represented. She has to stand on her chair so the judges can see her. She doesn't say that we secretly hate our team name.

Dr. Yee has everybody clap for us. He scans the room again. His voice drops. "Now, let's hear from Team ThisIsADumbChallenge."

Ramón, Missy-Bella, Titus, and two other sportsters—Addy Robinson and Yoshi Endo—stand. The sportsters do a fancy bob-weave-dab dance. Ramón looks like he'd rather be getting a cavity filled.

"Nice to see y'all have confidence," Dr. Campbell says. "Let's be sure we've got this right. Yer sayin' ThisIsA-DumbChallenge is your official team name?"

Most of Team ThisIsADumbChallenge do another bob-weave-dab. Ramón rolls his eyes.

"Well, whoa-nelly then." That must be western-speak for *you guys are so not going to like what's coming.* "If I recall correctly, and I always do, your name was supposed to give us some insight into what makes y'all special. Y'all knew that, right?"

"Well, yeah," Missy-Bella says. "But we figured you wouldn't mind if we had some fun."

They mind. Dr. Yee frowns. Mr. Montanari tosses his beard over one shoulder.

"I told you we should stick with the rules," Ramón hisses. "But no! You had to make a statement, Missy-Bella."

"Don't blame me! We all agreed."

The judges put their heads together. They whisper. They don't look pleased. Dr. Campbell makes a gesture that looks like a stop sign. Mr. Montanari waves his hands.

"I say corral 'em." Dr. Campbell wasn't kidding about being a tough judge.

ThisIsADumbChallege start to fidget. Yoshi rocks from one foot to the other like he's guarding a field hockey net and already knows he can't block the ball.

"Um, so you know what, Dr. Yee," Addy whines. She grabs a bunch of her blue-streaked braids and twists them together nervously. "Maybe we could have a second chance or something? It's only the first day of eliminations. My dad's going to freak if I get bounced in an early round."

"Mine, too." Yoshi looks seriously unhappy. "I knew I should have joined a different team."

Dr. Yee looks up from the judges' huddle long enough to shake his head. "Nope. This is a real competition, remember? No do-overs." He turns back to the judges but speaks up so we all can hear. "So we're agreed then?"

The DOM, Dr. Campbell, and Mr. Montanari answer together. "We are."

Dr. Yee shakes his head at the team who pilfered our seats in row JJ. "Team ThisIsADumbChallenge, the rules are clear. Your task was to create a name that enlightens and informs. Unfortunately, ThisIsADumbChallenge does not tell us anything about you."

He hoists his iPad like Thor raising his hammer to the sky. "Team ThisIsADumbChallenge, you failed to follow directions for this task. As a result, you are disqualified. Retake your seats. At the end of assembly, you and any other teams who don't make it through will begin your fun and rewarding community service project with Mrs. Jalil."

CHAPTER 13

Frederick Douglass Zezzmer

Whoa! Nobody says anything for at least one whole minute. Then the buzz starts.

"Did that just happen?"

"Missy-Bella's sooooo mad."

"Don't tell anybody 'cause I like to keep a low profile in competitions, but I'm going to win STEAMS!"

"What about your team?"

"Eh, they're duds. But I've got this. They won't slow me down."

The good news for ThisIsADumbChallenge is that they aren't the only ones who end up being disqualified. Six other teams get sacked for not following directions. Dr. Yee gives a lecture about being mindful about what we call ourselves "because you will always live up—or down—to your own expectations."

Then The DOM does a pile on. She likes quotes as much as Dr. Yee.

"Eleanor Roosevelt once said, 'No one can make you feel inferior without your consent.'" The DOM hits a superhero CEO pose and scans the room. When she gets to me, I feel like she looks me right in the eye. I can't help myself. I sit up straight. "That means *you* decide whether or not to listen to people determined to make you feel bad," The DOM says. "So if you're calling yourself something that means you're less than anyone else, *change the message in your head!*"

For the record, my folks think the same way. This one time, Julius told Pops he couldn't run his playlist at our house because the songs were full of the n-word. He wasn't having it. Pops was all set to argue, but he took a look at Julius's face and, for once, decided to let it go.

Turns out, the kids who didn't follow the naming directions will also have plenty of company in Mrs. Jalil's office. Three more teams get bounced because they uploaded their names after the deadline. Dr. Yee doesn't accept WeBelieveInPrizesForParticipation's argument that posting their name at 10:15 P.M. shouldn't count as a fail, because it was only 9:15 P.M. in California, and besides, 10:15 P.M. yesterday hasn't even happened yet for countries that are east of the International Date Line.

"You get an A for imagination, though." Dr. Yee winks at The DOM. "A lot like us, am I right?"

"It's not even noon, and ten teams are out already," one of Team FriendsSincePreschool says. "I thought this contest was going to be easy."

After wrapping up the review of team names, Dr. Yee has the disqualified teams stay in the auditorium for a special talk. Everybody else is dismissed to homeroom, where we'll get details about this afternoon's challenge.

I snail-walk backwards so I can watch and listen as long as possible. Who knows what I'll learn. Secret STEAMS scoop that can only be shared after kids get bounced, maybe? I let the other kids stream around me.

"Listen up, kids." Dr. Yee plops on the edge of the stage so he's closer to eye level with the eliminated teams. Or at least he would be if all their heads weren't down. "Thomas Edison supposedly said that instead of failing, he found ten thousand ways that won't work. That's amazing! Look how much he accomplished. If Edison can keep going after thousands of mistakes, you can keep going after one." Dr. Yee flashes the Vulcan hand salute. "Don't be sad that you didn't make it past the elimination round. Use this experience to get better. Let's talk about how."

Something good's coming. Too bad I don't get to hear it. One of the TallerThanOurGrandpas steps on my toes as we near the door. Then somebody spins me around. Somebody else shoves my back. The next thing I know, I'm in the lobby, and smack in the middle of an All-TheElsas pep talk.

"This is serious," Elsa D. says. My stomach gets in the way of her elbow as she loops arms with Elsa T., Elsa T^2, Elsa R., and Elsa V. "Elsas, I don't care who we have to crush this afternoon. We will not get eliminated today."

The Elsas aren't the only team on fire. Do-Re-We-Win are harmonizing on a battle song. A group of mathatrons called TheTriangleLites write equations in the air to calculate the odds of beating TheNeverLastonians and WeDreamAboutFlying. WeDoNOTLikeEachOther! cheer as they decide to stop not-liking each other long enough to win.

I call my team into a huddle. For some reason, The Shark is still carting her backpack. It's probably like a security blanket.

"I'll carry it." Liam loops the straps of his duffel—which is crammed with tennis balls, golf balls, a collapsible golf club, swimming goggles, one of those plastic whatevers for badminton, a martial arts yellow belt, and a bag of green marbles—over his shoulder.

The Shark eyes him suspiciously. Except for a few hisses and growls yesterday, she hasn't had much to say. Rumor has it, she's about to skip another two or three grades.

Liam must be trying to get on her good side since they'll start high school together.

"I won't drop it," Liam promises.

I wait for The Shark to launch a zinger. She surprises me though. She shrugs out of the backpack and hands it over. "Thanks."

Then, she smiles.

Who knew she could do that?

The lobby clears faster than usual. Everybody ignores the weather which, lucky for us, is photo-perfect blue skies so far.

We race up the path to homeroom. I barely touch pavers for George Washington Carver, Rachel Fuller Brown, and S. Joseph Begun I'm going so fast.

I'm ahead of The Shark, which is understandable. She's nine. Her legs are short. And I'm ahead of Huey. Padgett and Liam zoom past me like I'm standing still, though. I don't think their feet even touch the pavers.

"So many stairs," Huey wheezes as we climb to the second floor. He's got one hand clamped over his shirt pocket so he doesn't lose his deck. Sweat drips from the tip of his nose. "I never noticed there were so many stairs. Why did Dr. Yee decide we need morning exercise again?" He groans when Coach Judy appears on the landing. She doesn't even look winded. "And how do teachers get up here so fast? There's nothing about how they do it in the student handbook. However they do it, I don't think it's fair."

The accordion doors are pulled back already so there's one giant homeroom. Kevin Gannon, who uses a wheelchair, and Spring Hollweg and her service dog, Beets, took the elevator. They're here already. Mr. Happy and Ms. Latrice are here, too.

Coach Judy ushers the rest of us inside. *TWEEEEP!!*
We zip.
"Sit with your teams, kids." *TWEEEEP!!*
We sit.
"The list of remaining teams has been updated." Ms. Latrice presses a remote. The team roster beams on the whiteboard.

I was expecting the disqualified teams to have skulls and crossbones in their spaces or at least have thick red lines through their names, but apparently Dr. Yee and the judges thought doing something that cool to show who blew the first test wouldn't be appropriate. The list is plain. It's just a little shorter.

AllTheElsas	TallerThanOur-Grandpas	
Do-Re-We-Win	$A^2 + B^2 = BeatU$	EmbraceTheNerd
TheExcellentorators	WeScareOurselves-Sometimes	WeDreamAbout-Flying

WeAllLikeGumdrops
We♥Math
Lil'Notes♪♪

MorePopQuizzesPlease
GirlsRockScience
TotallyUnstoppable
We'llFixGlobalWarming
IxnayOnTheBodySpray
FriendsSincePreschool
StraightThroughTheGoalPosts
MakerSpaceDemons
NeverEverEverGiveUp

TravLiUeyPadgeyZezz
TheTriangleLites
TheImprovAbles
WeBeB-BChampions
TheMightyCraftyCraftonizers
WeDoNOTLikeEachOther!
VegansRTougherThanUThink
Waiting4OurGrowthSpurt
StillCan'tOpenOurLockers😵
1OfUsLostAGerbilIn2ndGrade

TheNeverLastonians
WeBelieveInYetis
We'reGoodAtRiddles
WeStudyRocks
Plié'sTheThing
SlightlySleepDeprived
Sportsters4Ever
NoGradingOnTheCurve
WeMayWimpOut
AlwaysOnTimeForClass!
SoMatureWeShouldBeInHighSchool

We mull the new competitive landscape as Coach Judy and Ms. Latrice use plastic hole punchers to update our cards.

S   T   E   A   M   S   !
becomes
S   T   E   A   M   S   ✳

Mr. Happy's in charge of leading the next part of the discussion. He stalks to the front of the room. He's wearing a hockey helmet, wrist guards, shin guards, and gloves, but he still looks worried.

"As you can surmise from my precautionary attire, this afternoon's competition is primarily an engineering challenge." He sighs and rolls his eyes toward the ceiling. "However, you will also get math credit for your work in this contest because you'll need to do some careful calculations to win."

We♥Math squeal. GirlsRockScience high-five each other. TheMightyCraftyCraftonizers and MakerSpace-Demons clap. Padgett grins.

IxnayOnTheBodySpray and TheExcellentorators seem worried.

"You will have two hours to complete this event," Mr. Happy says. "It will be held at Ruth Gates Pond by the lower school. After you fill an environmentally friendly, animal-safe balloon with water, your task will be to create a device that will successfully transport said balloon across the pond." He pauses for a second.

That's it? This challenge is no problem! The middle school maker space has tongue depressors, microengines, wires and, rubber bands. I can use those to make a drone capable of carrying a balloon all the way across the pond.

Everybody knows inventing is my special talent. I can ace this challenge by myself.

I pull out my notebook and start sketching. I'm not the only one getting an advance start. NeverEverEver-GiveUp are making a mock prototype of a . . . I don't know what that is, with their shoes.

Mr. Happy sighs. "I see some of you are already coming up with ideas for your device." He shakes his head as the Elsas start air-designing with their fingers. "I encourage you to remember that this is a team competition. Everyone in your group must have input. And also, there's no need to get ahead of yourselves. We've taken the liberty of creating a box for each team with directions and all the supplies you'll need. I don't have to tell you to read the directions carefully."

Nobody stops planning. One of the NeverEverEver-GiveUps slumps down in her chair and uses her feet to snag a We'llFixGlobalWarming kid's shoe. AllTheElsas's air design gets so big that Elsa D. and Elsa T^2 push three of the SlightlySleepDeprived kids aside to make room. My sketch is a thing of beauty: a five-piece balloon launcher with pre-calculated weight projections. I wish I could pat myself on the back.

"Hey, Mr. Happy. Can't we just kick the balloon across the pond?" Farrow asks. "I can send it over like a field goal." His team, TheExcellentorators, fall over laughing.

Now that I'm finished with my sketch, I'm itching to ask a real question, but The Shark beats me. Her hand shoots up like fireworks on the Fourth of July.

"If you're giving us supplies and directions, does that mean we're all making the same thing? How will we get bonus points for design and ingenuity?"

That's what I wanted to know! Does The Shark have her own Operation DazzleYee underway?

"Leave it to The Shark to want extra credit," somebody behind me breathes.

"She's like that in every class," someone else grumbles. "She gets extra credit on everything. How can somebody that small collect so many A's?"

"There are no bonus points in this challenge." Mr. Happy answers.

Seriously?

"So unfair!" Elsa V. hisses.

Cherub looks like she got a plate of navel lint for lunch.

I stop breathing. No bonus points for my balloon launcher? I'm never going to impress Dr. Yee at this rate! My head thonks on my desk.

"Your devices will either succeed or they will fail." Mr. Happy clearly doesn't care about our devastating disappointment. I'll bet he's delighted to skip having to figure out the difference between A, A+, and A++ grades for a whole week. "Those whose devices fail will exit the competition. The last ten teams to finish the competition may be disqualified, too. Eliminated teams will spend the rest of the week with Mrs. Jalil, who should be starting the fun and rewarding community service activity"—he checks his watch—"right about now."

CHAPTER 14

Mrs. Jalil

A magpie sits in a tree right outside my office window. A squirrel nibbles a crust of bread on a sidewalk nearby. A tiny rabbit hops across the grass.

It's so serene and quiet. That's what I love about Benjamin Banneker. I always get so much done while students are in class.

So far today, I've already submitted the purchase order for a new hot spot—and a temporary, limited-function flip phone—for Padgett Babineaux. It can't be easy living in the same motel where her grandmother works, riding the city bus to school every day, keeping all those difficulties bottled up inside her, and having virtually no friends. But her schoolwork never suffers. And she's truly a delightful girl. A little hyperfocused, maybe, but at Benjamin Banneker, who's not?

I take a sip of tea—chamomile with honey and a sliver of lemon—and open the folder on my desktop where I'm storing essays from students who want to attend Benjamin Banneker next year.

When I worked at my previous school, Exemplar Academy, prospective students generally wrote admission essays about family, pets, their favorite subjects, and their most beloved teachers.

Students applying here write about things like time travel theory and reversing climate change. One student submitted an essay about creating a life-size model of the human musculature system out of Jell-O. (He included pictures. I will never eat red Jell-O again.) Douglass Zezzmer wrote about becoming the world's greatest inventor. Travis Elizabeth Cod wrote about creating an environmentally resistant biosphere to sustain life on Mars. She was five.

I don't see many essays about non-STEM subjects anymore—not even from the arts students and the kids who are most excited about sports. I think parents assume their children need a STEM-related essay to stand out. That's not correct. I'm most interested in essays that reveal children's real passions.

I take another sip of tea. It's so yummy. Perhaps I'll brew a second cup when the first students eliminated from the STEAMS competition arrive.

I'm sure they'll be disheartened. They'll want to reflect quietly. I planned a nice, low-key activity for them: helping me stuff welcome packets and goodie bags for the families who come to our open house next week.

"Hey, Mrs. Jalil!" An eighth grader named Candace Swawola pops her head in my office. She has blond hair and dimples. She also has the pent-up power of a thousand suns. "We're here to start our service project. Are you ready for us?"

"Us?" What am I hearing the hall behind Candace? It sounds like the stomps of a college marching band. I'm getting a bad feeling. "H-h-how many are coming?" When Dr. Yee outlined plans for the STEAMS competition before spring break, he was certain only one or two teams would be eliminated on the first morning.

"Oooo, a whole bunch of us," Candace coos. "Probably fifty. That first challenge was really tricky."

"Fifty?" I sputter.

"Umm-hmmm. At first, we were really disappointed. We would've been fine sitting in your office all day filing papers and stuff. But then Dr. Yee said some of the world's most successful people bounced back from failure. Dr. Yee said we have to motivate-motivate-motivate ourselves to keep going. Dr. Yee said we can accomplish anything if we charge ahead with purpose. Now, we're all revved up!"

Oh my. This isn't good. These kids will finish stuffing welcome packets and goodie bags in about fifteen seconds. Benjamin Banneker students do not like being bored. They'll look for anything to keep busy.

I wonder where Dr. Yee is. I really, really, really want to talk to him! I predict we'll have a spirited conversation. And also, I need teacher reinforcements. If I get a running start, maybe I can open my window and escape outside.

Too late! Candace waves over her shoulder. I'm barely on my feet before an entire herd of middle schoolers tries to cram through my door.

"Dude, watch out! You're standing on my foot!"

"Stop breathing on me!"

"Ewwww, Madeline! Aim your farts in another direction."

"Hi, Mrs. Jalil! Are you happy to see me?"

"What do I have to do to get an A in this service project?"

There's no way they're going to fit through the doorway. Not all at once. But that doesn't stop them. They're literally climbing over each other trying to get in.

"It's Dr. Yee's fault we're here so early."

"Right! That first challenge was so unfair."

"I know I just got here, but can I go to the bathroom?"

"Do you have any candy, Mrs. Jalil?"

"I think I'm allergic to paper. I self-diagnosed using a chart I found online."

I sink back into my chair, trying not to hyperventilate.

"You're pulling my haaaaair!"

"Madeline, I swear if you fart again, I'm going to scream!"

"She who smelt it, dealt it, Regina!"

"Can I play some music, Mrs. Jalil? I have a playlist."

"Do you have 'U C Me B-N U' by Open Wounds? I cry every time I hear it. I play it all the time."

"Are you okay, Mrs. Jalil? You don't look so good."

CHAPTER 15

Frederick Douglass Zezzmer

I t's weird how fast we adapt when things change.

Yesterday's lunch was awful. There was too much anxiety about who we had to sit with and where we were supposed to eat. Today, we've settled into a new normal.

Most of us anyway. WeDoNOTLikeEachOther!'s truce didn't last long. They look at us with, I dunno, admiration, as we cruise through Stump 'Em B4 You Lunch 'Em. We're almost as fast as TheExcellentorators, and that team clicks like a well-oiled machine.

It helps that today's Stump 'Em is easy: Name and describe a fish species found in the Arctic. Each of us gets our question right.

Once we get our food—wild-caught or vegan fish sticks, salad, and potato puffs—we drag two extra chairs to a table by the window. Originally, the table was set up for three people. It works fine for five when we all scrunch in.

"We need a plan to ace this afternoon's challenge." Padgett taps her index finger against her temple. Until this week, I'd never seen her eat in the cafeteria. She's always in lunchtime detention with Mrs. Jalil. At least, that's what I heard.

"I'm down for game plans." Liam rubs his hands together. "Game plans are the secret to winning in football. In most sports, actually."

We stare at him. He doesn't notice that we're skeptical. He crams two fish sticks in his mouth sideways. If swallowing without chewing was an Olympic sport, Liam would get the gold.

"So listen, I think I should be the lead for TravLiUey-PadgeyZezz today," Padgett says. "No offense to anybody, but Mr. Happy said this would be an engineering and math contest. I'm already taking an intro to physics class. I study a lot of math and engineering principles there." She looks me in the eye. "What do you think?"

Not that, that's for sure. In my plan, *I'm* the leader. TravLiUeyPadgeyZezz wins because of me. Dr. Yee almost cries when he asks me to represent B-B at GadgetCon. The rest is history.

"Doug!"

My perfect daydream evaporates. "What?"

Padgett flicks her retainer. "I said, what do you think about my idea to lead the team this afternoon? It makes sense, right?" She leans in with her eyebrows up. She smiles slowly and I get a closeup view of her retainer.

I can't finish Operation DazzleYee if I wind up in the hospital after getting Babineauxed. But I can't just give in either.

"Uh . . . what if we're co-leads for the first contest? That's a good compromise, right?"

Padgett makes a face. "I'm the one who's winning the Nobel Prize in Physics."

"You haven't won it yet!"

So much for the happy new normal. Huey looks from me, to Padgett, to me again like we're his parents. Liam scoots away from the table and buses his tray. The Shark keeps eating like nothing's happening. She's either doing an astronaut-in-training meditation or not paying attention because of the noise. When life gets hard, it helps to be an expert at blocking things out.

Huey and I are the only ones who walk back from the cafeteria together. TravLiUeyPadgeyZezz fell apart completely during lunch. Padgett left because she said she had to send an email from the library. Liam went to the gym for a pickup hoops game with other sportsters. The Shark said she was going to stay in the cafeteria and read a textbook.

"What are you going to do about T.W.'s paper?" Huey asks. "Not to nitpick or anything, but STEAMS isn't just about you getting picked for GadgetCon anymore." He stops by Günter Blobel and Ellison Onizuka's pavers, folds his arms, and rocks back on his heels. "Now that I figured out that Grandpa would want me to use STEAMS to forget about my stage fright, I need to make sure you don't have to bail on the team because T.W. glues your head to a pillow or something."

"I've got the paper covered," I boast. It's hard not to puff out my chest. "It only has to be five pages. I programmed DougApp to analyze online articles about Shakespeare and draft a report that sounds like T.W. Minus all the *uh*s, *um*s, and 'eat my fist, Mr. Big Brain' stuff. And since DougApp is doing the writing, I'm not cheating."

Huey crinkles his nose and twists his head like Barack Opawsma does when he's confused by a cat toy. "I don't think that's how it works." He pops his arms into a superhero CEO pose like The DOM. Then he narrows his eyes into slits. He sucks in a breath and holds it. He sticks his neck out. His face starts to turn red. What is happening?

"I'm not cheating *technically*," I say, trying to stay calm. "It's what Moms would call a gray area. That's what I'm banking on, anyway."

"Anything else?" Huey wheezes.

"Yeah." I scratch my head. "What are you doing?" I motion at his superhero stance. "Is this, like, you being uber competitive or something?"

"Whew!" Huey blows out his breath in a whoosh and almost falls over. He drops his hands to his knees. "You caught that, right?" he squeaks. "Cool! I'm getting better then. I've been practicing being tough and steely and only focused on me. That's how I'll finally beat my stage fright. Like Grandpa said, 'say cheers to fears!'"

"Uh . . . okay." Since I don't want to say Huey actually looked like he was going to pass out, I point to where Susan La Flesche Picotte's paver marks the place where the path heads to the lower school instead. "The next STEAMS challenge starts in ten minutes at the pond. Race you down?" Huey's still gasping. He creeps forward like a really old man. "Or maybe we just walk."

I don't know what I'm expecting to see when we get to the pond. But definitely not this. *Sweet great-grandmother Jones!* Forty-one boxes sit side by side near Ruth Gates Pond's west shore.

TravLiUeyPadgeyZezz reunites for the challenge. Sort of. We know we have to work together, but, except for Huey and me, we stand at least an arm's length apart.

We're not the only ones squabbling either. I don't think FriendsSincePreschool are even talking anymore.

Dr. Yee walks up with Mr. Montanari and Dr. Campbell. He must be telling them about B-B's campus because they keep looking around like kids in a ice cream shop. They point at different buildings and talk over each other to ask questions. The DOM isn't with them so I guess she must have already gone back to work. Mr. Happy, Ms. Latrice, and Coach Judy are monitoring the shore on the side of the pond opposite from us.

"As Mr. Happy explained this morning, this will be a timed challenge. You'll have two hours for this test," Dr. Yee says. He rubs his hands nervously instead of giving us a Vulcan hand salute. "Your goal is to create a tool capable of transporting a water-filled balloon to the east side of Ruth Gates Pond. Each box contains five balloons. Try different options, but make sure you have a working device by the time you reach your last balloon. If none of your balloons reaches the other side of the pond before the competition ends, you will be eliminated."

We wind up between TheExcellentorators and AllTheElsas. TheExcellentorators glare at us. Seriously, this team is so in sync it's amazing. They don't even have to speak. They use some kind of telepathic mind meld to coordinate their group evil eye.

StillCan'tOpenOurLockers😵 grab a box without reading the directions and wade across the pond. "Done!" Brutus Smiley yells.

"I don't think that's right." Huey grabs the rules sheet from our box. "These directions don't tell us how to build our devices exactly." He flips the paper over. "But they do say the balloon has to be on, in, or propelled by a constructed device to cross the pond." He squints at the page. "Oh, and we can't just make a boat and pull the balloon across either."

"Welp, count StillCan'tOpenOurLockers😵 out then." The Shark turns our box over and dumps out the rest of our supplies. We have a bag of rubber bands, the balloons, a bag of LEGO, a rock, a plastic gardening hand trowel, a roll of duct tape, and a package of thin wood rods.

It's not the equipment I imagined when I sketched a plan during homeroom, but I can work with this. "I'll make a catapult," I announce. "I've made plenty of them before."

"No. *I'll* make a catapult." Padgett scowls. "Effective catapults rely on the basic principles of physics. Stored energy. Velocity. That's how it's done."

"I know that."

"Well, you didn't say it. I said it. And I'm the leader."

"Nobody said you're the leader."

Padgett and I go at each other for a while. Then The Shark clears her throat. "I sketched plans for a catapult while you were fighting." She points to a diagram in the sand. "We'll use the LEGO to build a base. The trowel will be the bucket. The rods will make the frame and the winch. The rock will be a counterweight. The rubber bands will store and release energy to launch the balloon."

"When did you—" I start.

"How did you—" Padgett interrupts.

"I'm an astronaut-in-training. I know stuff," The Shark smirks. "And by the way, since I came up with the plan, I guess I'm the leader for this challenge, huh?"

Padgett takes out her retainer and flicks it menacingly. Then she laughs. "Yeah. I guess you are." She gives me an embarrassed side-eye then grabs the LEGO bag and tosses it to me. "She showed us, didn't she?"

No point in arguing—we've already wasted enough time. I drop to my knees and start assembling the base, following The Shark's instructions. I pass the rods to Padgett and she builds the frame.

Our internal teacher alert goes off and we both spot Dr. Yee watching us from nearby. He studies us, looks down and taps something on his iPad, then studies us again. Look. Tap. Look. Tap. He must be making notes about GadgetCon!

Padgett and I start silent-competing on who can build their part of the catapult first. Padgett's fast, but thanks to all the years I've spent making gadgets, I'm faster. Operation DazzleYee is on a roll!

The Shark ignores us. "Not good," she mutters. She pats the dirt in front of our construction site. "It's too bumpy. We need a flat foundation for our catapult. Whoever finishes first needs to help smash this down. Our catapult won't work otherwise." She looks around. "Hey, Huey!" she calls. "Want to help with construction?"

AllTheElsas and TheExcellentorators go quiet. The spotlight's on Huey big time. I look up just as his stage fright blows back like a hurricane.

"Keep going." I shove my supplies at Padgett. "I'll be right back." I bound over to Huey and pull him into a quick huddle. "Do you want to do construction?"

"Nah. Not really" he mumbles. He kicks the ground. " I was thinking maybe I'd double check the rules and track time and stuff."

"Cool."

We break huddle just as Padgett throws up her arms and yells, "Done!" She grins at Dr. Yee. He smiles back. Then he rushes off to stop a water fight between WeAllLikeGumdrops and SlightlySleepDeprived.

Huey wanders off too. I think he's scoping out the competition.

Padgett's hard at work pounding the foundation with one of her clogs when I get back to finish the base.

"What about me?" Liam asks.

The Shark doesn't hear him. She's flopped on her belly, inspecting the base I constructed.

I look at Padgett. She looks at me. For two people who were dead set on leading TravLiUeyPadgeyZezz a few minutes ago, we're being awfully nice to each other now.

"What do you think?" I ask.

"What do *you* think?"

"I was thinking maybe . . . the catcher?"

"Ha! What a coincidence. So was I."

"That's great!" Liam digs into his duffel and pulls out a catcher's mitt. "Put me in, Coach. I'm ready!"

Ritchie punches Farrow when Liam runs to the other side of Ruth Gates Pond and bounces around on his toes. "Can you believe it, Farr? Liam's going to be a catcher. He hasn't caught anything since second grade!" He laughs so hard he falls on his back.

Padgett stops her construction project long enough to glare. "What did you say?"

Ritchie chokes on his laughter. "Nothing!" He grabs a handful of rods and tosses them to Pixie. "I don't have time to say anything, Padgett. I'm helping TheExcellentorators build a boat."

"That was nice," The Shark mumbles when Padgett squats down next to me to help fasten rubber bands to the frame. After we finish that task, we tape some rods together to make the stop plate for our catapult. We use our hands as protractors to make sure the launch arm stops at exactly ninety degrees. If that angle worked for the ancient Romans, it's good enough for the STEAMS engineering and math contest.

"Hey guys, I've got an update!" Huey charges over. Now that he's not in the spotlight, I think he's feeling better again. "Four teams have been disqualified for not following directions. StillCan'tOpenOurLockers☺, SlightlySleepDeprived, 1OfUsLostAGerbilIn2ndGrade, and—wait for it—Sportsters4Ever. They taped all of their wood together to make a baseball bat, filled a balloon with water, then tried to knock it across the pond like they were hitting a home run. They kept trying the same thing over and over again. By the time they decided to do something different, all of their balloons were gone. They wanted a second chance, but . . ."

"No do-overs!" Padgett, The Shark, and I say together.

"Also, twelve teams have already succeeded," Huey reports. "You'll never believe what TheNeverLastonians did! They built a raft out of the wood rods, put a balloon on the raft, and one of them waded through the water making waves to sail it across. It was d-i-s-g-u-s-t-i-n-g! I think Cherub hurled. Do you know how many ducks poop in that pond each year?"

"Probably twenty. But that's still a lot. No way we're going to risk getting duck poop in our hair." Farrow butts in from a few feet away. Who knew he was listening? Who knew he even watched ducks?

I watch Farrow lead TheExcellentorators to the pond with their boat. I have to look. It floats, but it doesn't go anywhere. Ha! They haven't figured propulsion yet.

"Therrrty min'uts!" Mr. Montanari calls. He and the other judges wander around checking progress and scanning for infractions of the rules. Thanks to Mr. Montanari's warning, all the remaining competitors kick into high gear. TheMightyCraftyCraftonizers send out scouts to see what the other teams are doing. WeBeB-BChampions has a meltdown.

Another thirteen teams—including TheExcellentorators—finish the challenge. They taped their spare wooden rods together, snuck to the narrowest part of the pond when I was the only one watching, and shoved their boat across the water with one push.

Suddenly, we're one of twelve teams left to compete. And ten of us may be automatically disqualified.

"Feef'teen min'uts!" Mr. Montanari announces. Time is flying by. I'm sweating so much, my glasses keep sliding down my nose.

We launch our TravLiUeyPadgeyZezz test balloons. The catapult works perfectly, but Liam misses catching the first two by a mile. It's like his feet want to go one way. His body wants to go another. And his arms have no clue. He yells, "Sorry! I'll get it next time," each time he blows it. But he doesn't.

"Tun min'uts!"

We try moving the catapult so Liam has more time for catching. Bad call. The third balloon goes a little wild. It soars over the bridge, across the field, and whacks Mr. Happy on the head.

"'Ey min'uts!"

We move our catapult back to its original position. Lil'Notes♪♪ made a catapult also. They sing an anthem composed for this challenge as their catapult launches.

Flyyyyyyyy, balloon. Flyyyyyyy.
Help us winnnnnn. Let us winnnnnn.
We should winnnnnn.
We'll smile thennnnnn.
Flyyyyyyy.

It's not the best music I've ever heard. But it works. Their balloon sails over the water and lands unbroken in a nest of jackets they made on the other side of the pond.

Things aren't looking great for the rest of us.

"Using Liam Murphy for a catcher is like launching a balloon at a pile of rocks," Ritchie shouts. He points at

Liam. "Same result! Splat!" He can barely talk, he's laughing so hard.

"I've got this one! I've got it for sure!" Liam calls. He pounds his fist into his catcher's glove. "Trust me! I won't let you down!"

"SPLAT!" Ritchie hoots. "S-p-l-a-a-a-a-t! SPLAT!"

"Let's do this!" I shout Ritchie down. I motion to The Shark to release the catapult. All of the teams who aren't competing run along the shore to find a spot to watch.

"I's li' a sta'pede o' th' wee' Shetland pooneees!" Mr. Montanari gurgles, forgetting to call the time. "O'er 'n unner 'n—oooh-ee up'n th' ayr!"

Our fourth balloon sails high over the pond. The Shark's aim is perfect. The arc is fantastic.

"I've got it!" Liam yells. "I've got it!" He gets right under the balloon. He frames his arms into a big, fat circle. The balloon drifts right to them. Then . . . it passes through them because Liam doesn't close his arms in time.

"Oooh," everyone says.

Our balloon smacks on the ground and shatters. Dr. Campbell shakes her head. "That there is what I call a mighty unfortunate occurrence."

"Good teamwork, though," Dr. Yee observes.

"Aye," Mr. Montanari says.

Farrow shrugs. "I guess that's the end of TravelyPaddlely . . ." I don't think he's being mean. He spends a lot of extra time with Ms. Latrice in the enhanced learning center, because remembering things is hard for him. I think he really forgot our name.

"Fur min'uts!"

The remaining competitors are frantic. NeverEverEver-GiveUp built a ballista that looks sturdy enough to launch a car. Something about their design is flawed, though. They've had three spectacular crashes. They're down to two balloons—one more than we have—when Jochen Cordel races to the edge of the pond and fills their fourth balloon almost to the brim with water. He uses a hollow rod to puff in huge breaths of air, probably to give it extra lift.

"That's enough!" Jochen's teammate Kiku Southcott warns.

Jochen ignores her. The balloon explodes when he tries to force another breath in. Abel O'Callaghan, another NeverEverEverGiveUper, collapses to the ground. "Oh my gawd! Jochen, what did you do?"

"We need a new plan!" I bark to my team.

Padgett's face goes flat. "I've got this!" She races around the shore to Liam, sky-blue clogs flying. She taps him out.

"Tha'rrrree min'uts!"

Back on our side, TheImprovAbles are pacing. They still have five balloons. They never tested a prototype. Their device looks like a miniature Viking ship. A water-filled balloon sits like a happy mermaid on its deck. Their rock is tied to a rod at the bow. It's like a figurehead. A really heavy figurehead. Their boat only gets about two feet offshore before it sinks.

Padgett gets in the ready position.

"'Oooo min'uts!"

Can Padgett even catch a balloon?

"Ah-woon min'ut!"

No time to worry about it. I make the call. Our balloon launches. Then the last NeverEverEverGivingUp balloon launches. They sail through the air, neck to neck.

"Ferty-fi' sec'unds!"

This isn't going to work. Our balloon is moving way too fast.

"Ferty sek'unds!"

Padgett takes off running. She trips. She almost falls. She kicks off her clogs and sprints barefoot.

A few feet from us, TheImprovAbles drain their boat, rip off the figurehead, fill another balloon, and try to throw their ship into the pond with brute strength. It disintegrates midair.

"Therrrty sek'unds!"

Our balloon starts to descend. Padgett makes an arm circle, just like Liam.

"Feef'teen sek'unds!"

NeverEverEverGiveUp's balloon is microinches behind ours.

"'Oooo sek'unds!"

With a quick jag to the side, Padgett gets under our balloon. She leaps in the air.

"Ah-woon sek'und!"

Then everything shifts to slow motion.

"An' tha's tyme!"

CHAPTER 16

Huey Linkmeyer

Doug's so tired, I think he goes to sleep with his eyes open while we wait for Mr. J. to pick us up. I'm drained, too. I'm pretty sure all my muscles have gone on strike or something. I can barely sit up.

First off, NeverEverEverGiveUp's balloon exploded on impact, but we had to wait for the judges to decide if Padgett caught our balloon before time ran out. Ritchie said Mr. Montanari ended the contest before she had possession. He was definitely not pleased when the judges ruled in our favor. He kept hissing, "I'm watching you" until Dr. Yee told him to settle down.

Second off, even though our bodies were exhausted and our brains were short-circuiting, we had to have "community come together time" after the contest. Dr. Yee used it to lecture us on healthy competition. Thanks to

Ritchie and some of the other kids, Dr. Yee was disappointed in our behavior during the last challenge. He made us recite B-B's school values while Mr. Happy, Ms. Latrice, and Coach Judy updated our punch cards.

S   T   E   A   M   S   ✹

is now

S   T   ✹   A   ✹   S   ✹

And third off, a total of fourteen teams were knocked out of STEAMS in this competition. Teams are dropping like flies!

"So how was the first full day of STEAMS?" Mr. J. asks when Doug and I stagger into the car. He takes a long sniff then rolls down the windows. "Pretty active, huh?"

Doug and I smell our pits.

Then we smell each other's pits.

Nothing. Well, maybe a *little* something. But it's not too bad. We look at each other and shrug.

"You would not believe how tough it was," Doug groans. "Dr. Yee says each challenge is supposed to engage our minds and our bodies." He makes air quotes around *engage our minds and our bodies*. "I think it's just another attempt to see how much our delicate nervous systems and psyches can take."

"Dr. Yee sent an email to parents with an updated team roster." Mr. J. pauses at a stop sign, then turns down a side street. "A lot of teams have been eliminated. Congratulations on making the cut."

Doug and I sigh in tandem. I pull out my phone and open MeU to recheck the updated list.

1. WeDreamAboutFlying
2. SoMatureWeShouldBeInHighSchool
3. MakerSpaceDemons
4. StraightThroughTheGoalPosts
5. AlwaysOnTimeForClass!
6. FriendsSincePreschool
7. Waiting4OurGrowthSpurt
8. WeMayWimpOut
9. VegansRTougherThanUThink
10. IxnayOnTheBodySpray
11. TheNeverLastonians
12. We'llFixGlobalWarming
13. WeDoNOTLikeEachOther!
14. TheMightyCraftyCraftonizers
15. TotallyUnstoppable
16. Plié'sTheThing
17. WeBeB-BChampions
18. GirlsRockScience

19. WeStudyRocks

20. TheExcellentorators

21. We♥Math

22. MorePopQuizzesPlease

23. Do-Re-We-Win

24. $A^2 + B^2 = BeatU$

25. TallerThanOurGrandpas

26. Lil'Notes♪♪♪

27. TravLiUeyPadgeyZezz

We made it. Barely.

Thinking about our close call is too much for Doug. His eyes close. His head thuds back on the headrest. A minute later, he's snoring.

Mr. J. turns the radio to his second favorite channel, something called Smooth Jazz. I don't know what smooth jazz is exactly, but one song sounds like all the others to me. They're easy to zone out to. Like listening to a car engine or watching a caterpillar crawl on a tree.

While Mr. J. drives down another side street, I scroll through the photos on my phone. My favorite is the one with me, Grandpa, all my parents, Doug, Doug's mom, Mr. J. and probably half of the people in Doug's neighborhood having a potluck barbecue in Doug's backyard. I make the photo a little bigger to check out the picnic tables: roasted corn, burgers and buns, different kinds of salads, and lots of desserts. My stomach growls just remembering how good the food was.

If I expand the photo even more and look really close, I can see the tip of Grandpa's magic card deck—now *my* magic card deck—peeking over the top of his shirt pocket.

But I don't make it bigger because, whenever I do, I also notice the big brown spots on Grandpa's hands, and how tired he looks, and how his mouth is droopy from his first stroke. He had a second stroke a few weeks after the photo was taken. After that, he had to move to Porch View for specialty care. He was only there a year before he died. I don't like remembering that.

My stomach rumbles again, but it's not because I'm hungry this time. I can't help wondering if Grandpa would be disappointed because I didn't do much to help my team out in STEAMS today. Even if he was, though, he wouldn't show it. He'd say, "Head up, kiddo. Say cheers to fears."

None of my parents know what that means either, but I'll figure it out one day.

All of this sad remembering is starting to give me a headache. I sigh and drop my phone back in my pocket. Mr. J. checks me in the rearview and smiles. I smile back. Then I stare out the window for the rest of the drive.

"We're home," Mr. J. says when we get to Doug's house. He gives the brakes a pump so the car bounces a little. Just enough to make sure we're both awake.

Doug doesn't live in a gated community like my dad and my second stepmom. And his room has bunk beds and posters of inventors on the walls, instead of two double beds and a gaming system like my room at Mom and Stepdad #2's.

I really like coming here, though. All of the homes on Doug's block have enormous old trees with knobby trunks in their front yards. And Doug's house has a bunch of other stuff that make it feel special. Like three hammocks in the backyard. And blueberry bushes and apple trees with fruit I can pull off and eat without asking. And a giant welcome mat on the front porch that looks like a sunflower. And a sign Mr. J. carved and put on their back gate that says,

We bought a house. We made a home.
Julius, Annie, Doug

Doug's next-door neighbor, Mr. Cohen, waves as he power-walks by. He reminds me of Grandpa when he was healthy.

Mr. Cohen does a quick spin at the corner then races back. He's wearing a shirt that says *Yoga is my superpower.*

When I FaceTimed Doug during the pandemic, I saw Mr. Cohen in the background a bunch of times showing Mr. J. how to do different poses.

"Hi-hi, neighbors." He gives Doug and Mr. J. friendly claps on their backs. "Hello, Hubert," he says to me. "Nice to see you."

"Love the shirt, Nate," Mr. J. says.

"I thought you'd like it. You've become quite the yoga fan."

"That I have. I had a great teacher."

"Thank you, son!" Mr. J. and Mr. Cohen aren't related—Doug told me that Mr. J. grew up in foster care and doesn't know his parents—but Mr. Cohen calls him son anyway. It makes Mr. J. smile every time.

"I ordered this shirt from a company in Toronto," Mr. Cohen says. "Actually, I ordered two. I left yours on your back porch."

"Thank you!" Mr. J. whoops like a little kid and scampers away.

"That's what I like to see. True dedication." Mr. Cohen smiles at us. "The shirt's not the only thing back there, boys. I did a little baking today."

That perks both of us up! We race to the backyard to see what's waiting.

CHAPTER 17

Frederick Douglass Zezzmer

Huey and I get our second wind after we help ourselves to the plate of soft, chewy, salted caramel–chocolate chip–peanut butter cookies that Mr. Cohen left with Julius's new shirt. Amazingly, starting with dessert does nothing to keep us from eating two servings of *you really don't want to know what's inside* stuffed ravioli.

Julius takes me aside in the hallway after dinner. "Annie texted while I was cooking. She said she's going to need a few more days to decide if she wants to take the promotion or start a business. She'll tell us more this evening." He blows out a breath. I do too. "Big life changes can be stressful, Doug," he tells me. "You're doing a good job supporting your mom."

When we go back in the kitchen, Julius announces that he's giving me a pass on doing the dishes. Then he makes

A LOT of not-so-subtle suggestions for Huey and me to clean ourselves up. Then he stops suggesting. When he launches into, "You boys reek. You're wilting my garden, and you're inside the house," Huey races upstairs to the bathroom while I feed Barack Opawsma.

When Huey comes down, he gets plug-the-electronics-in-the-downstairs-chargers duty while I take my shower. Full disclosure: my clothes smell way worse when I get out of the shower than I thought they did when I got in.

I stuff them in a trash bag and shove it in my closet. The clothes will be fine in a week or two.

We've got a couple of hours until Moms calls for her FaceTime, so Huey and I decide to strategize for tomorrow's STEAMS contest in my room.

"You know why the other teams smoked us today?" I swig the last of my grape juice, stash the glass in my underwear drawer so I don't forget it—there's already a crusty saucer in there; who knew?—and climb to the top bunk. Barack Opawsma does one of his world-famous leaps and snuggles beside me for a rub.

Huey plops on the floor. He opens his duffel. "They're better at math and engineering?"

"Noooo." I throw my pillow at him. It bonks his head. "They have one clear leader. One Captain Kirk. TravLiUey-PadgeyZezz has five. Or at least three: me, Padgett, and The Shark. We debate everything. That slows us down."

Huey shrugs. "We made mistakes today, but we learned stuff." He pulls out his dirty-clothes bag. It's like an oversize Zip-Lock. Completely spill, dust, dirt, and smell proof. "Forgot to roll up my socks before I put them in here," he explains. His second stepdad doesn't like it when Huey puts unrolled socks in their hamper. It's his laundry rule.

I don't have smeller-vision, obviously, so I don't actually see the cloud of sweaty-STEAMS-challenge-clothes stink that mushrooms out when Huey opens his bag. It's impossible to ignore, though. Particularly when Barack Opawsma soars off the bed like a cannonball and runs into the hall yowling.

If Huey's dirty-clothes bag is a barometer, maybe the clothes I stuffed in the back of my closet will need an extra month to cure . . .

Huey reseals his laundry bag superfast. "Oh man, that's awful. It's making my eyes water. I think I'll roll them up tomorrow." He sniffs and wipes his nose. "But speaking of tomorrow, how hard do you think Wednesday's challenge will be? I think it'll be massive. I'm getting major *Lord of the Flies* vibes from the judges."

I happen to be an expert on that book. "*Lord of the Flies* doesn't take place in Colorado."

"It could."

"But it doesn't."

"But it could."

"Doug." *Holy cow!* I almost have a heart attack. Julius has perfected his stealth parent mode over the years. I never hear him coming. He grins proudly from the bedroom door and waggles my phone and laptop.

"Your father's on FaceTime for you. He said something about you offering to tutor T.W. again."

"Oh yeah. Yep. Yes. Absolutely." I'm only lying a little. And technically, so is Pops. We both know I didn't offer. But still, guilt takes over. I can't meet Julius's eyes. Neither can Huey.

Fortunately, Julius doesn't notice. "Well, that's good. I'm glad you're helping your stepbrother." He hands over my electronics and pats my shoulder. "Here you go. I put Elliott on hold so you have a minute to set up. Have a good conversation. I'm going to work in the garden for a while. I'll be back before Annie calls." He clomps down the stairs.

Pops is taking the FaceTime call from his computer. He doesn't realize he's sharing his screen. So he also doesn't know that, in addition to seeing him, I can see his Greg G. checklist and tip sheet, and the digital sticky notes he keeps for the book he wants to write in a few years. He already has the title: *Gridiron Parenting.*

"Hey, Pops."

He must suddenly realize what he's been sharing. The image wobbles while he fiddles with his computer then his face fills my screen. I get a close-up view of nose hair before he leans back and gives me a full view of his den. The wall behind his desk is full of framed photos. *Pops in his Broncos uniform. Pops getting a trophy. Pops getting another trophy. T.W. getting a trophy.* The cabinet in the corner holds some of the actual trophy hardware. It's packed.

Pops scans my room, too. He told me once that he can't wait to see the football jersey he gave me hanging on the wall. It's not up yet. I'll get to it eventually.

Pops sighs. He must have had a long day. He sounds tired. "Hi, son." His eyes wander to the side. Probably scoping out his checklist. He looks back at me and gets right to the point. "I understand you haven't spoken with T.W. about his paper yet."

T.W. emerges and glowers at me in the background. "Haven't gotten a text. Haven't gotten an email. Haven't gotten a call." Even his freckles look mad.

"It's very important you two finish that paper on time, and that T.W. does well," Pops says.

I try to check myself before I do an eye roll. Too late. I catch Pops's glare. "I'm sorry. I've been busy with—"

"My paper's on Shakespeare," T.W. butts in.

"I know it's on Shakespeare!" My fists clench.

"So how come you haven't done anything yet? I thought you were smart, Mr. Big Brain."

"I am smart!" *Smart enough to off-load your stupid paper to DougApp*, is what I want to say.

Pops's gaze goes up and down. Then down and up. He must be scanning the tip sheet. It throws him when T.W. and I go at each other. He's not like Julius. This one time, Pops and Patrice had T.W. stay with us when they had to go out of town for a weekend, and T.W. started arguing about who rake the leaves and who would scoop them into the trashcan. Julius got right between the two of us and told us to knock it off. He used his "do not test me voice." (For the record, we didn't.)

Greg G. doesn't have a "one size fits all" solution for stepbrother hate, so Pops shushes us with a wave.

"This is what you need to understand, Doug," he says, leaning in close to the screen. "Helping T.W. get a good grade is your top priority."

"But . . ."

"I know you don't have classes this week. You can focus on the paper exclusively. Understood?" He gives me the EZ stare. *That didn't take long.*

"He can't, Mr. Zezzmer!" Huey blurts. "Doug has a deadline, too. Our team has to win STEAMS."

I was hoping Pops would have remembered STEAMS on his own. From the look on his face, he forgot. No surprise.

"Huey's right, Pops," I say. "It's like I told you yesterday. STEAMS is a contest for the entire middle school. My team is going to win. Then Dr. Yee will pick me for GadgetCon. It'll be like"—I try to find the common ground Moms always talks about—"one of your best touchdowns!"

I can literally feel Huey flinch beside me. Pops shakes his head. "We talked about this already, Doug."

My face gets so hot it must be glowing. I know we talked about it. Why can't Pops remember what we said? And how did we get into another angry bumper car conversation so fast?

I inhale deeply, the way Julius does when he practices yoga. Then I speak extra slow: "You said GadgetCon wasn't a sure thing. But it *will* be a sure thing after I win STEAMS."

Pops groans. "Please, no more talk about GadgetCon. You can go to that anytime."

"But I don't want to go anytime! I want to go *this year*! I have a plan!"

"No, I have a plan!" Pops actually yells. He pokes his screen with his finger and hits me with a look that's ten times worse than the EZ stare. It's awful. I stop breathing. And moving. I totally freeze up. "How many times do I have to tell you that I made a plan for your life the day you were born?" Pops demands. "Why can't you just follow it?"

It's a good thing the phone volume's low. And it's a better thing that Julius is in the garden. If he heard Pops shout like this, he'd fly up the stairs.

Everybody goes silent. Huey's mouth drops open. Then he tiptoes across my bedroom and shuts the door.

"I'm sorry. I shouldn't have shouted." Pops looks embarrassed. "What I'm trying to say, Doug, is that it's a beautiful thing when parents can pass something on to their children. I know you have my athleticism somewhere. I'm only pushing you so it comes out."

He holds out his hands like he's making an offering. His eyes are still mad, but at least he manages the EZ stare grin again. I guess that's better than nothing. "Listen, let's make a deal," Pops says. "If you win STEAMS and get picked for GadgetCon, we'll have another conversation. Summer sports camp is still at the top of the list, but check these three boxes—finish T.W.'s paper, win STEAMS, and get picked for GadgetCon—and maybe we can figure out how you can do both."

I sigh. "Sure, Pops."

"Thank you." Pops sounds exhausted. "We'll talk again tomorrow." And then he's gone.

"Are you okay?" Huey asks. He opens the door. Good move. Even though our clothes are sealed in bags, the stench of today's STEAMS sweat is starting to seep out. We need more air.

I've heard Huey's parents and steps argue plenty of times, so I'm not too embarrassed by what happened with Pops. But I still feel like there's an avalanche happening in my stomach, and I don't like that at all.

When Pops came back, he expected us to be a family immediately—but it's not working. I don't know him. And he doesn't know me. What am I supposed to do with that?

"Dude," Huey taps my shoulder. "Seriously, are you okay?"

"Yeah." And I am. Because after that conversation, I'm more determined than ever to get to GadgetCon.

"The first thing we'll do is finish T.W.'s dumb paper." I grab my laptop and activate DougApp. It's been churning away since yesterday. A draft of the paper is already done.

"How does it look?" Huey peers over my shoulder.

"It's fine." I scroll through the paper. "Shakespeare was born . . . blah blah blah. He wrote a bunch of stuff . . . blah blah blah. I like him because . . . blah blah blah. And then he died . . ."

"I know. Blah blah blah," Huey says. "Do you think it's, um, kind of flat? I think it's flat and . . . I have a very high tolerance for flatitude. That's what Mr. Happy says, anyway. Well, that's sort of what he says. Basically, he says most of my papers are flat."

"It may be flat, but it's good enough for T.W." I'm so steamed at my lazy stepbrother. The way I see it, he's the one responsible for this latest trouble with Pops. One day, I'm going to do something that takes him down. "If we were going to make it snazzy, you know what I'd do?" I make a copy of the paper, save it, and delete the intro. "Right here, see? Instead of saying, *Following is a thoughtful reflection of the many contributions William Shakespeare made to European, nay, global literature,* we would give this report an honest-to-goodness T.W. spin. That would serve him right."

"How?"

"Like this." I pound the keys for a full five minutes. When I stop, I lean back, so Huey can see the screen.

"Whoa! Are you serious?" He reads the new text aloud. *"Everybody's heard of William Shakespeare, but did you know he also wrote under a pen name? He did! I learned that by doing lots of research. All by myself. For the reals. So instead of writing about the same old, boring stuff as everyone else, my paper is about the works of William Shakespeare's alias, the one and only Wills B. Speare.* Dude! That's golden!" Huey grabs my laptop. He types, stops, looks at the ceiling, types, and then hands the laptop back.

I read his contributions. *"I'm going to write my very impressive report about Wills B. Speare's top three plays. You may have heard of them: Romeo & Cleopatra, Juliet Caesar, and Hamlet MacMarybeth."* I snort grape juice through my nose. "You're a comedy genius, Huey."

It's my turn now. I hunch over my laptop and type some more. We keep going like this for an hour: writing, reading, trading the laptop back and forth, and giggling so hard that Julius comes up to see what's going on. I didn't even hear him come inside.

"Nothing," I say, when he asks what we're doing.

Julius squints at me, unconvinced.

"No, seriously. We're just goofing around. We're rewriting the works of Shakespeare." I read one of the fake quotes from *Hamlet MacMarybeth*. "*Double double toil and trouble. Why's my name so weird? Do I live in a bubble?* I think STEAMS is making us silly."

Julius smirks. "Okay. Fine." He holds up a warning finger. Guess what? I don't freeze up. "Twenty more minutes," Julius continues. "After that, laptop's off. Connect both it and your phone to the chargers downstairs."

We finish the fake paper in half that time. It's five pages of brilliance. I hate to delete it. We'll probably never come up with something this good again.

"I'm going to save it," I declare. "When we're old and forgetful—like, when we graduate college or something— we can reread this for fun." I press the Command and S keys.

"Should we check T.W.'s real paper against the assignment directions before we stop?" Huey asks. "I think we should—double-checking is good."

"You worry too much, Huey. T.W.'s paper is saved in the cloud, not my laptop. There's full separation." I tap in a few more commands for DougApp and flip the laptop closed. "Besides, the only other task for DougApp is to scan the real paper for typos one last time and email it to T.W." I hop off the bed and head to my door.

I have an idea. Probably my best idea ever. At least for today.

"Wanna check for leftover cookies when we take the electronics downstairs?"

CHAPTER 18

T.W. Jackson-Zezzmer

J-Z!"

Ugh. Mr. Arbor keeps tabs on at least two dozen kids at Northeast Den, but they never get called into his office as much as I do. It's so great being special.

"I expected an update on your English paper first thing this morning." Mr. Arbor crosses his arms. "Well?"

I sag into my normal chair. "I'm on it."

"Tell me you at least read the Shakespeare plays."

"I at least read the Shakespeare plays." That kind of snark would usually get a laugh. But not today. Ms. Hamilton must really be on his case about me. "Don't stress, Mr. Arbor. I'm set." And it's true. An email landed in my inbox this morning. I haven't opened it yet, but I know what it is. Elliott came down hard on Mr. Big Brain last night.

Mr. Arbor looks relieved. Being a guidance counselor must come with a ton of grief. "Okay then."

I push out of the chair. "Can I go now?"

It's Wednesday, which is *Let's chat about what gets you excited about learning* day. But Mr. Arbor waves me out instead of leaning back to talk about new science fiction books. A few minutes later, I scuttle into an empty classroom and open Mr. Big Brain's email on my laptop.

To: TWJZ
From: TheRealDealDoug
Here.

Guess those are all the warm fuzzies I'll get from Stepbruh. It's better than nothing. And he put a good title on the attachment, *William Shakespeare: A Literary Legend.* That works. I'm sure it'll get an A, just like the report on *The Three Musketeers.*

I don't bother reading the paper after I download it. There are more important things to do. I open the Benjamin Banneker website, click on the application page, and key in the password for the account I set up. The cursor goes right to the spot that's always stumped me.

3. Students: Upload an essay about a subject that interests you. (Note, completing this step will automatically forward your materials to the admission committee.)

I upload the Shakespeare paper and hit the submit button. That's it. Done! Everything's starting to come together.

I pull out the sci-fi book I brought in today. I yanked it from my stash without looking.

Turns out, I picked one of Rick Riordan's Kane Chronicles novels. It's fantasy, not real sci-fi, but I still like it. If they ever make a movie, they need to hire me to do stunts for whoever plays Carter Kane. I know the story by heart.

I suppose I could send the Shakespeare paper to Ms. Hamilton now instead of reading, but . . . nah. That can wait until tomorrow. Ms. Hamilton couldn't handle getting an assignment from me two days early anyway. Thursday's soon enough.

Besides, uploading that essay to Benjamin Banneker's admission page was like lifting a two-ton elephant off my head. I kind of wish Mr. Big Brain—okay, *D-o-u-g*—was here instead of doing that stupid STEAMS competition. He's the reason I've got spark again.

CHAPTER 19

Frederick Douglass Zezzmer

Good morning, Benjamin Banneker middle schoolers!"
Dr. Yee jogs onto the stage from the wings. Dr. Campbell and Mr. Montanari trail behind him. They sink into their director chairs slowly. They don't look awake yet, but Dr. Yee is full of energy. He gives us the Vulcan hand salute. He's in a great mood.

Huey and I are in great moods, too. Not only is T.W.'s paper finished, but now that Missy-Bella and the ThisIsADumbChallengers have been banished to wherever it is that eliminated teams go during assembly, we're back in row JJ.

Huey pats the armrest of his regular chair like it's a puppy. "Home sweet home."

Padgett climbs over our legs to claim the seat next to me. She says, "Morning."

Huey and I answer, "Hey."

The three of us shift to the left and lift our feet so The Shark can squeeze by and get to the fourth seat when she comes in. Everybody says "Hi" to each other.

Huey and I pretend not to notice that The Shark's hair is back in its usual ridiculously lopsided ponytails. We look at the ceiling. Padgett leans down and whispers in The Shark's ear.

The Shark blinks like her brain went to Mars without her. Then her body catches up to wherever her mind went. She whispers back, "Daddy's still learning."

Then Padgett whispers, "My grams only had boys before me. She had to learn too. It took forever."

Huey pokes me. "Why are they whispering?" he whispers. "We're right here. We can hear everything."

Padgett glares at us. She flicks her retainer. We zip and go back to looking at the ceiling.

Padgett whispers to The Shark, "I can probably fix it. I mean, I can try . . . if you want."

"Really? Thank you!" The Shark forgets to whisper. Then she grins. I don't think I'll ever get used to that.

The Shark whips around so her back is to Padgett. They giggle and laugh while Padgett straightens her ponytails.

Liam clambers in last. He takes chair number five. He must still be humiliated from the catapult challenge—he barely speaks. He keeps his head down so his hair covers his eyes. He sinks even lower in his chair when TheExcellentorators stomp into the row behind us.

"I'm still watching you, TravLiUeyPadgeyZezz," Ritchie hisses. "You should have been disqualified yesterday." He whacks Liam's head with his ID card. "Particularly you. You're the *I got it! I got it! Nope, I dropped it!* boy."

All of TravLiUeyPadgeyZezz whirls around to give Ritchie a team glare. Padgett flicks her retainer. But then . . . wait for it . . . Farrow punches Ritchie hard on the arm. "Stop."

"What!" Ritchie rubs the punch spot.

"It's first thing in the morning, dude. Give him a break."

Farrow smiles at Padgett, braces gleaming. His hair is parted on the side. The small section is slicked down. The bigger section is teased way, way, way up. It's like he tried to sculpt it into a ski slope. How did he even get it to do that? He must've been up all night working on his head art.

Huey ankle-bomps me. "Dude, close your mouth."

"But his hair . . ."

Padgett smiles back at Farrow.

This is getting weird. I ankle-bomp Huey. "Are you seeing this? What's happening?"

"How is everyone feeling today? STEAMS is getting exciting, am I right?" Dr. Yee calls out. Somebody quiet-whoops. Dr. Yee scans the room. "I heard that, Ramón!

Thanks for checking in. Now, head over to the main building. We have a special morning presentation planned for all teams not in competition. Everybody, give it up for Ramón!"

Someone darts from the back of the room while we clap. Whoever it was moved so fast I couldn't see them. I wonder if it really was Ramón. No, it couldn't be . . .

"Remaining teams, if you checked the roster on MeU last night, you saw that it said twenty-seven teams were still in the competition after yesterday's challenge. But if you looked before assembly, you noticed the number is now twenty-four," Dr. Yee says. "Unfortunately, three teams—SoMatureWeShouldBeInHighSchool, StraightThroughTheGoalPosts, and TotallyUnstoppable—had to withdraw due to, um, unforeseen circumstances." He lowers his head like he's in mourning, but the corners of his mouth twitch when the whispers start.

"They went to Mighty Meat Burger last night to celebrate."

"Eating there is NEVER a good idea."

"I heard they all got the squirts. Uh, that means diarrhea, Evian."

"I know what it means, Marvel. Jeez."

"Eew, that's so gross! Why would they even tell anyone?"

"If it happened to me, I would for sure keep it private. But you know what? This one time, when I was on vacation . . ."

Dr. Yee clasps his hands behind his back and rocks back and forth—heels to toes, heels to toes—until the chatter dies down. He's not being impatient. I kind of think he likes listening to us blab. Who knows why?

"We're going to change the pace this morning to help our judges reacclimate to being in school," Dr. Yee announces.

"Mighty sportin' of you," Dr. Campbell says. She rubs her eyes with her fists and yawns. She's doing better than Mr. Montanari, though. His head lists sideways. His man-bun is wilted. His hands twitch like he's dreaming. Dr. Campbell nudges him with her foot.

Mr. Montanari jerks up with a loud snore. "Noo aslee'! Jus' thee'kin'."

"We have four remaining challenges: science, technology, arts, and sports," Dr. Yee says. He's so excited, he can't stand still. I can't help but puff my chest out a little. Not to boast or anything, but I'm all-around awesome in STEM. If we do science or technology today, I'm the obvious choice to lead.

"This afternoon, we'll have an unconventional science challenge," Dr. Yee continues. I throw my arms up and Ramón-whoop. Dr. Yee smiles. "Why thank you, Douglass."

The rest of TravLiUeyPadgeyZezz—well, everybody except Liam—laughs.

"What was that?" Huey asks.

"Just happy. I love science."

Dr. Yee zooms into full-on lecture mode. "I invite you to remember that many scientific discoveries come from having infinite curiosity about the world around us." He paces the length of the stage. "Discoveries happen when we're open to seeing things we often ignore or take for granted in new and different ways."

Yep. I knew that.

"Today, you'll experience what occurs when—and if—you can harness the power of your team to pursue a common goal."

Yep. I've got this.

"Since our high school students are away on a field trip, we're going to use their science building for our afternoon challenge." Even Liam lifts his head at that. Middle schoolers never get to go into high school buildings. That sanctuary is off-limits. Go in without permission . . . you may never come out.

"Keep in mind, high school is all about choices," Dr. Yee says. He makes a bunch of fake check marks in the air. "Trust me, you'll have opportunities to make plenty of choices today. But before we learn more about the science challenge, we're going to hear from a surprise guest speaker. Let's give a rousing Benjamin Banneker welcome to my dear friend and mentor, Dr. Nell Tubman!"

He claps. I jump up and clap, too. Way to show I'm listening! Dr. Yee sees me and nods. Check another box on the Operation DazzleYee scorecard. But then other kids catch on. There's a spontaneous clapping competition. A few rows down, Winnie and her team of uber techno-vengers clap with their hands *and* their feet. Some of them even thump their heads together. Soon the auditorium is filled with applause. I clap until my hands burn. It doesn't matter. Dr. Yee knows who got things started.

"Well, that was unexpected, but I'll take it," he says when the claps die down. "Now, about Dr. Tubman. She worked at the National Department of Standardized Educational Testing for many years. Several of the annual assessment tests you take are the result of her efforts."

"That's supposed to make us happy?" JoJo mutters behind us. "I hate assessment tests."

"Dr. Tubman retired recently, so she's not here to revise testing protocols," Dr. Yee says. "But she has wonderful stories to share about how questions are selected. If there's time, I'll ask her to tell you why she chose oval instead of square bubbles for the answer sheets. It's so fascinating!" He's totally gushing. "B-B middle schoolers, give it up for Dr. Nell Tubman!"

A tiny, gray-haired woman wearing a red plaid dress and black tights walks to the podium. "Good morning, children."

"Oh no," Huey breathes. "She called us children."

She did. My brain goes numb.

"I love observing how young people use their minds these days," Dr. Tubman says. She tugs a tablet out of her pocket. "Before I start my little talk, why don't we do a few logic questions? Won't that be fun?"

Ann-Ruth Park from WeBeB-BChampions jumps up. "Will these questions count toward an elimination?"

"That's a great idea!" Pernell Ramirez from More-PopQuizzesPlease says.

"Ooo' my," Mr. Montanari moans. "'ere we go now."

"I think it's a good idea, too! Make it an elimination, Let's knock some teams off the leaderboard," Ollie Bartholomew from $A^2 + B^2 = BeatU$ calls. He swivels his head like a periscope. "If you're not part of $A^2 + B^2 = BeatU$, you're going dowwwnnnn!"

"You see, this is what I tried to tell you . . ." Dr. Yee whisper-shouts to his mentor, but she smiles and shushes him, and claps her hands.

Dr. Yee steps aside. He bows his head, defeated. "Dr. Tubman, you have the floor."

"Such wonderful energy. I love it!" Dr. Tubman pumps her fists in the air. "Kids, your voices have been heard. I don't really understand this challenge. But . . . I decree this to be an elimination round, whatever that means!"

CHAPTER 20

Padgett Babineaux

From: babineauxp
To: grams

Grammy!
    I know it's only ten o'clock. Sorry for sending your afternoon blood pressure pill reminder so early. A lot's happening today. I may not be able to send another email until late.
    Guess what. Dr. Yee brought in a guest speaker. She had us do a logic problem elimination. I LOVE logic problems! So does Travis. So does Doug. We were on fire!
    The whole competition was wild. Kids were jumping and screaming. It was like a reality show. A bunch

more teams got knocked out. Only eighteen teams left now! We're not last anymore either. I copied the list for you. Check it ooooout! We're up to #4!

1. WeDreamAboutFlying
2. MakerSpaceDemons
3. Waiting4OurGrowthSpurt
4. TravLiUeyPadgeyZezz
5. WeMayWimpOut
6. VegansRTougherThanUThink
7. IxnayOnTheBodySpray
8. TheNeverLastonians
9. TheMightyCraftyCraftonizers
10. Plié'sTheThing
11. WeBeB-BChampions
12. TheExcellentorators
13. We♥Math
14. MorePopQuizzesPlease
15. Do-Re-We-Win
16. $A^2 + B^2 = BeatU$
17. TallerThanOurGrandpas
18. Lil'Notes♪♪

Did you notice we're way ahead of TheExcellentorators? I know I said they were awful last night. But now that I know them a little better, I think they may not be so bad after all. At least not all of them, anyway.

So that's what's happened so far this morning. Everything's going so fast.

Isn't it weird how time speeds up when life gets exciting?

CHAPTER 21

Mrs. Jalil

Things I've learned from Benjamin Banneker's STEAMS competition (so far):

1. All the words to "U C Me B-N U" by Open Wounds.
2. All the other songs on Open Wounds's debut album. ("Will You Be My Headache?" speaks to me.)
3. That I shouldn't assume Benjamin Banneker students are joking if they ask to make rocket fuel from coffee grounds using a recipe they found online. They *will* try.
4. That Benjamin Banneker students should never, EVER be allowed to get bored.

"Wow, Mrs. Jalil, you've really kept us busy." Candace leads a pack of muddy, disheveled students into my office. "Who knew there were so many trees on campus? How come nobody thought about counting them before?"

It's hard to believe these students were on competing teams just two days ago. They barely knew each other. Now, they're working together. Maybe, just maybe, Dr. Yee had a good idea with STEAMS.

I'll admit, I had a bit of a panic attack when so many children surged into my office yesterday. But there's a reason I got an A in event coordination during assistant principal training. I know how to make a plan!

I have the students who've been eliminated from the competition doing dozens of different tasks. In addition to those working with Candace, one group is in the computer lab developing a new design for our website. Another group is down in the lower school, building robots in the maker space room with the younger kids. A third group is on a video call with students at a school in Kampala with Dr. Addo. A fourth group is talking with students in Haeundae with Dr. Chun. And a final group is on their way to a senior center with Coach Judy to sing and dance.

So far, I've managed to keep 32 teams—160 students—happy and busy. As long as there're no surprises or disruptions, I've got this handled. My "I can survive STEAMS" schedule is perfect. Nothing beats a well-thought-out plan!

"Sooo, what do you want us to do now, Mrs. Jalil?" Candace drops a nearly empty packet of colored ribbons on my desk. "We counted, categorized, and marked all the trees. There were more than three hundred."

Wait. What? "I-I thought you were just coming in for a break."

"Oh no. We figured out how to make the tree-marking project go a lot faster. We broke into subteams and sub-subteams. Then we borrowed one of the drones from the maker space room for aerial mapping. That really sped things up. We made a spreadsheet and everything. We're done!"

"But . . ."

"I'm boooored!" Malia Whitney moans.

"Me too," somebody else says. I think it's Cruz Lolly. His admission essay said he's going to make a transporter beam that works for humans before he turns twenty-five.

Just then, Latrice staggers into my office. She looks like she's been in a hurricane. Her shoes are untied. Her clothes are wrinkled. Her faculty ID card is tangled in her hair.

"Assembly . . ." Her mouth quivers. "There was a special, unplanned elimination in assembly. More teams are coming in a few minutes. But first"—her voice breaks—"Dr. Yee is giving them a high-energy pep talk."

"Oooo, Ms. Latrice!" Candace squeals. "Look everybody. It's Ms. Latrice. I'll bet she's got something for us to do!"

We challenge Candace's group and the kids on the newly eliminated teams to go to the library and write ten kid-friendly, how-to-code tip sheets for schools in Denver that don't have a technology program. Whoever finishes first will win . . . *something*. We have to figure out a prize.

"How long do you think that'll keep them busy?" Latrice asks. Coming up with mind-benders for Benjamin Banneker students is exhausting. She plops on top of an air purifier. She doesn't have enough energy to walk to my guest chair.

"Probably less than three hours. We'll have to come up with something new for them after lunch." I slump into the chair behind my desk. "Honestly, I'm out of practical ideas. Maybe we should have them find a way to harness a supernova."

Latrice giggles. "We should have them try it in Dr. Yee's office. It's bigger."

I imagine the mess they'll make and laugh too. "After what we've been through this week, there's no way he can complain."

I make tea for both of us: hibiscus, sweetened with honeyed ginger, and topped with thin slices of lime.

"How're you doing with admission requests from interested families?" Latrice asks. Openings for Benjamin Banneker's upcoming school year always fill before November. But instead of having a waiting list, we save twelve spaces—one for each grade—until spring and give highly motivated children a final chance to apply. Some of our brightest, most interesting students—kids like Padgett Babineaux, who somehow find the courage to go after what they want, even though the odds are not in their favor—arrive that way.

Unfortunately, I haven't started reading student essays yet. STEAMS is taking a lot of time.

Latrice drains her cup and hops to her feet. She's obviously fortified and full of energy again. Oh, the joy of being young.

"Tell you what. I'll make the rounds and check on the students," Latrice says. She bounces on her toes. "You get started reading essays while it's quiet." She jogs off.

I sort application essays into all the usual categories: lower school, middle school, high school; those from kids who will be the first in their families to attend Benjamin Banneker; those from children of alumni; and those from kids who have a sibling who's currently a student here.

The sibling applications are my personal favorite. Sometimes prospective students are excited to talk about their families. Sometimes they don't say anything at all. Fortunately, it's easy to figure out who belongs to whom by cross-referencing parents' and guardians' names. That's how I discover the application for Terrell Wallace Jackson-Zezzmer.

I didn't know Douglass had a stepbrother. He never talks about him. I wonder if Terrell is another inventor. If so, I wonder if he's equally fearless. Memories of how Douglass's fifth-grade invention, the FredZezz Spray-On Dirt Evaporator, almost made his pants disintegrate during lunch flood my brain. That was a bit of a disaster.

I scan Terrell's application form quickly. He doesn't mention anything about inventing. In the space for interests, he writes *science fiction, sports* . . . and *Shakespeare.*

My goodness. That's quite brave. Declaring a love for centuries-old literature takes courage. Luckily, it's fine when kids are different at Benjamin Banneker. Not everyone wants to be the world's greatest inventor, win the Nobel Prize in Physics, make a working transporter, or be the first person to walk on Mars.

Some people may find it boring, but I think a nuts-and-bolts essay about one of history's most famous writers will be fascinating. I open the essay and settle back to enjoy some scholarly text.

"William Shakespeare: A Literary Legend" by Terrell Wallace Jackson-Zezzmer

Great! I love it already.

Everybody's heard of William Shakespeare, but did you know he also wrote under a pen name? He did! I learned that by doing lots of research. All by myself. For the reals.

Hmm . . . Terrell didn't mention anything about comedy on his application. Maybe his submission just has a rough beginning. I scroll to the middle of the essay.

People wonder how Wills B. Speare wrote so many plays. I couldn't find an answer that everyone agreed with but, personally, I think it could have been time travel.

Uh-oh.

CHAPTER 22

T.W. Jackson-Zezzmer

I probably do an extra three thousand steps ducking through hallways and taking the long way to my classes so I don't bump into Mr. Arbor. All that weaving and bobbing doesn't bother me though. I'm floating. Seriously. I could take off and fly.

I get that submitting the Shakespeare paper for homework *and* for the Banneker application is double cheating. But this is the last time I lean on Mr. Big Brain . . . uh, Doug . . . to get my stuff done. I'll work harder when I get to Banneker. I'll pay attention in classes. Do my own homework. I may even ask Doug to show me how he writes such good papers. And I'll stop bouncing my football on his head. I'll show him my secret sci-fi stash since he likes reading too. I'll help him with sports. We'll start doing stuff together like brothers. I know exactly how things will play out. Way better than good.

Sooner or later, I'm going to have to tell Ma and Elliott about applying to Banneker though. Lucky for me, Banneker won't contact them until I get accepted. Good thing, I've got a plan. First, I'll knock everyone's socks off in sports camp and get recruited by the best club teams. There'll be a major competition for me. It'll be a preview of when all the DI colleges recruit me and I'm the top pick in the NFL draft.

Then I'll get my acceptance letter. Once I convince Ma to back me on changing schools, we'll talk with Elliott together. He won't be happy that I went behind his back, but I'm pretty sure he'll come around after I've proved that my ball game won't suffer, and I'm still headed to the pros.

Pretty much the only thing that has to happen for sure is that Ma and Elliott hear about Benjamin Banneker from me. But first, time for another boring lecture about William Shakespeare.

Today Ms. Hamilton starts off reading love poems called sonnets. They're impossible to figure out. Like, there's one that begins, *Shall I compare thee to a summer day?* I'm thinking Shakespeare's girlfriend must've been, like, "Honestly, dude, I do not care. If comparing me to weather makes you happy, you do you. But otherwise, what's the point?" My brain cells are turning to cement.

"Terrell, are you with us?"

Oh come on. Not again. "I'm sorry, Ms. Hamilton. I didn't hear you."

She pops her fists on her hips. Her go-to position when she talks to me. "Class, would someone like to brief Terrell on what we were talking about while he was daydreaming?"

Sure enough, Kamiyah Bean does her usual jack-in-the-box routine. She's on her feet before anyone else can get a hand up. "Ms. Hamilton gave us additional background on what she wants to see in our critique papers. The papers that are due on Friday. You know Friday? It's the day after tomorrow." *Please stop.* She doesn't. "Ms. Hamilton said writing a critique is like writing a well-researched, thoughtful movie review. She said we should present our unique perspective about why we find Shakespeare's works meaningful or why we don't."

If it was me who actually wrote the paper instead of Doug, my unique perspective would be, "No way! Shakespeare's not meaningful to me at all. I mean, some of the plays are kind of interesting. I like the ones with sword fights, witches, and stuff, but I like science-fiction books a whole lot more. No matter how tough things are in the real world, sci-fi gives me some other place to go. To the future. To the bottom of the ocean. To outer space. To different galaxies and different worlds. I could read sci-fi for hours. Shakespeare puts me to sleep."

But that's just me talking. I'll have to check the paper to see what Doug said I said. For all I know, he said I think Shakespeare is da' bomb.

"That's a wonderful summary, Kamiyah," Ms. Hamilton says.

Of course she does.

Kamiyah smiles and floats back to her chair. *Shall I compare thee to a summer day, Kamiyah?* Only if it's hurricane season and you're an incoming storm.

My eyes must've gone vacant again because Ms. Hamilton zeros in on me like a heat-seeking missile. "Terrell, at this point, I'd be interested to hear about the approach you're taking with your paper. What would you like to share?"

Man, this is why I hate Ms. Hamilton's "no technology in the classroom" policy. I could really use my laptop. Without it, I have no idea what my paper's about.

"I, uh." I check out the ceiling like I did when I got in trouble as a little kid. No answers then. No answers now. "I'm still doing research, Ms. Hamilton. Collecting my thoughts and whatnot. You know."

Ms. Hamilton doesn't buy it. She leans in, ready to take me down.

Lucky for me, the end-of-period bell rings. I'm saved from more humiliation. I'm out of my seat and through the door like a comet. The first thing I'm going to do when I get to my locker is grab my laptop and turn in that stupid paper so Ms. Hamilton will leave me alone.

"J-Z!"

I hit the skids. I barely remember what it felt like to be light as air. Facing Mr. Arbor after fifty-five minutes of Ms. Hamilton totally weighs me down.

"How was English today?" Mr. Arbor asks.

"Umph." I hop from one foot to the other. The old *better let this kid go or he's going to pee himself* trick.

"Your paper's going to be on time, right?"

"Umph." I hop faster. A bunch of tenth-grade girls stare at me and giggle. I totally don't care.

"Well, uh, that's good work then." Mr. Arbor looks seriously uncomfortable. If I weren't so heavily into my acting, and if Ms. Hamilton didn't make us leave our electronics in our lockers for English class, I'd use the camera on my phone to take a snap.

"Just make sure to do your best on this paper. And see me right away if you need help. Remember, you need to pass this class to avoid summer school. I know you can do it, J-Z!" Mr. Arbor whirls and heads to his office at warp speed.

I snag my tech as soon as I open my locker, fully intending to send my paper to Ms. Hamilton in the next ninety seconds. Before I do, I take a quick look at my phone out of habit.

Weird. My voice mail is full. I don't recognize the number on the first message. I hope nobody's in the hospital. I hit play.

Hi, Terrell. This is Mrs. Jalil from Benjamin Banneker College Prep. I'm calling because I read your essay this morning. It's . . . very unusual. Perhaps you sent it to me by mistake? Please call me back when you have a moment.

What the—? I play the second voice mail.

Hi, Terrell. It's Mrs. Jalil. Ignore my previous message. I wasn't considering the fact that you're in school today! There's no need to call me back. I can reach you another way. You neglected to put your parents' phone numbers on the application form, but fortunately, thanks to your stepbrother's student records, Mr. Zezzmer's contact information is already in our database. I'll give him a call right now. Have a wonderful day!

I can't wrap my brain around what's happening. I hit the floor—right there in the hall, right by my locker—and yank my laptop open. My computer desktop's kind of messy so I have to hunt for the Shakespeare paper. *Not it. Not it. Not it. There it is!*

There's got to be a mistake. Maybe the file got corrupted. Once I figure it out, I can fix it.

I start reading the paper. What is this? *William Shakespeare's alias? Wills B. Speare? Juliet Caesar? Hamlet Mac-Marybeth?* What's going on?

Then my phone buzzes with an incoming text.

Elliott: T.W., this is important! I'm about to call you. When you hear your phone ring, answer it!

CHAPTER 23

Frederick Douglass Zezzmer

Even though it's pizza day, I let the rest of TravLiUey-PadgeyZezz run to the cafeteria ahead of me.

I'm still wrapping my brain around having our next STEAMS challenge in the high school science building. It has a dedicated workspace for inventors called the Innovation Lab. And a conference room for visits with the professional STEMers who built our school. And a presentation space where the top students demo their projects for potential investors once a year.

B-B high school is another big step on my way to becoming the World's Greatest Inventor. Maybe I'll meet some of the kids who are also going to GadgetCon.

"Deep in thought, Douglass?"

Holy cow! I almost jump out of my skin. Dr. Yee apparently has the same stealth superpower as Moms, Julius, and most of my teachers. He falls into step beside me. Kids immediately swerve out of the way. I get a ton of *What-did-you-do?* eyebrow questions, and also some serious smirks and side-eyes.

"Nothing makes you more popular than walking with the principal," Dr. Yee says. "Trust me, I know. I had a lot of walks to the lunchroom with my principal when I was in middle school."

Yikes! What am I supposed to say to that?

Apparently, Dr. Yee doesn't notice me gulping. "So how are you feeling about STEAMS?"

"Um . . ." *Why can't I think faster?* This is a big Operation DazzleYee moment. I feel like my brain turned into pudding. And I don't even like pudding. *Aw man!*

"I don't think I've ever seen you at a loss for words before, Douglass," Dr. Yee says. "Don't be shy. Tell me what you think."

"Well . . ." Deciding what to do when grown-ups ask for your opinion is stressful. Are you supposed to tell the truth? Agree even if you don't? Fake a sneezing attack and run away?

This walk is taking forever. We're barely halfway to the lunchroom. Dr. Yee obviously isn't going anywhere. Maybe this is a test to see if I'm ready to join the high schoolers representing B-B at GadgetCon.

I suck in a breath and blurt out my answer. "To tell the truth, I wasn't sure about the challenges at first. I didn't understand why we had to have unconventional contests. We could have done more standardized tests, math Olympics, science fairs, hackathons. We're used to those. We do them all the time. But then I figured out that giving us something we're not used to was kind of the point. And I decided I'm okay with the contests after all, especially since TravLiUeyPadgeyZezz is so close to winning."

"I see." Dr. Yee nods thoughtfully. Points for me! My answer must have scored big. "Your team's performance is very impressive. You must have a good leader. Who's in charge?"

Huh. How am I supposed to take credit for being the leader *and* talk about cooperation, collaboration, teamwork, and B-B values at the same time? If I don't say I'm in charge, how will he know I can hold my own at GadgetCon? But if I skip over the warm fuzzy part . . . will he assume I ignored everything he said in assembly?

"Is that a trick question?" Dr. Yee laughs. *Oh no.* Did I say that out loud? "I mean . . ."

"Don't worry, Douglass. It wasn't a test. You know, I could have given a talk during an assembly about being a leader, but most of you wouldn't have listened, am I right?"

"Umm."

"Rhetorical question. No need to answer. The thing is, there's a big difference between saying you're in charge, and being a good leader. Anybody can do the first one. For the second, you have to try your hardest to do what's best for your project, what's best for you, *and* what's best for your team. Sometimes, those aren't easy choices. Get it?"

Truth: Noooo.

What I say is: "Yes."

Dr. Yee inhales like he's getting ready to launch into a five-part lecture, but he's out of luck. We're at the cafeteria doors. I get rescue-swarmed by my team. Dr. Yee wanders away.

I'm not sure I earned another check mark on the Operation DazzleYee scorecard during that conversation. I never got the nerve to ask if Dr. Yee planned to pick me for GadgetCon, and he didn't say. But he did pick me to walk to lunch with. That's a good sign. Once I ace this next challenge, I'll be his only choice.

"Liam's whole family is doing Stump 'Em today," Travis says as we group-walk inside. Whoa—hold up. I forgot to call her The Shark. Eh, whatever.

"They're doing word problems. Hard word problems." Padgett points to the ticker. *Students: 37. Parents: 51.*

Liam is still moping. His hands are shoved deep in his pockets. His head is down. I wonder if he told his parents about dropping most of our balloons yesterday.

"Stand back, everybody! Greatness coming through. TheExcellentorators in the house!" It's Ritchie. He's coming up fast behind us.

Liam tries to make himself smaller.

"We've got this." I push Liam in front of me. In front of Huey. In front of Padgett. In front of Travis. Now we're all between him and Ritchie.

"Who do you think you are, captain of the dweebazoids?" Ritchie demands.

I don't bother answering. We all want to help Liam. Once I got us started, everybody knew what to do. And now Ritchie doesn't have a chance to say any more. We're at the front of the Stump 'Em line.

"This must be Team TravLiUeyPadgeyZezz. Let's see if I get this right," Liam's dad says. He has a blue baseball cap with m stitched on the front crammed on his head.

"Really, Dad?" Liam groans.

Mr. Murphy isn't bothered. He's as cheery as Santa Claus. He points to each of us in reverse order to how we're standing. "Doug. Huey. Padgett. Travis. And of course, my favorite and only son, Liam. Welcome, kids. We've heard so much about you."

Liam's mom and sisters are blond, too. Just like Liam and his dad. And they're all wearing baseball caps. Mrs. Murphy's has ur stitched on the front. The tallest girl's hat has a PH. Her hair is pulled into a ponytail that hangs out of the hole in the back. The other girl's hair is cut short. Her cap says Y. From the sour look on her face, I think she'd rather it say WHY?

I feel for Liam. Having your family show up for Stump 'Em wearing baseball caps that spell out your last name is . . . rough.

"We've got everybody's favorite for lunch today: Pizza!" Mr. Murphy blares.

Mrs. Murphy and Liam's sisters point to the different varieties like they're working on a game show. It's all the usual choices: Meat. Double meat. Veggie. Veggie with pineapple. Meat with pineapple. Just pineapple. Vegan. Gluten free.

Even though they're athletes, Liam's mom and sisters eventually get tired of pointing.

"As you may have heard, we came up with some fun word problems for each team to solve together," Liam's mom says. She flashes a toothy smile.

Liam's sister in the Y cap rolls her eyes. "Math is never fun, Mom."

"Don't overgeneralize, Stephanie," Liam's mom chides. "Some people love math."

Liam's dad pops a piece of paper into a clipboard placed on a menu holder just for today's Stump 'Em. "Here's an oldie but goodie for you kids. It's about two people who have a business presentation in Chicago at four P.M. tomorrow. Person A plans to take a westbound plane that travels at . . ."

Travis elbows past Liam so her nose is about an inch from the paper. She reads it for herself, then plucks a pencil from behind her ear and starts scribbling numbers on a napkin.

I've got a question. "Is Person A pre-cleared for boarding or will they have to wait in the general security line? We have to factor the wait into the travel time."

"Word," Huey says. "And will Person A have to check bags? Checking bags can take forever. Also, four P.M. is really late for a meeting. What if Person A isn't an afternoon person? I'm not an afternoon person. It's rough for everybody. Just ask Mr. Happy."

Padgett raises her hand. "Is this a one-day presentation? If so, why doesn't Person A do a video call? Shouldn't Person A be thinking about their carbon footprint? Aren't they concerned about climate change?"

Liam finally looks up. "A video call would be better for the environment. Mom and Dad, can we change the question?"

"Um . . ." Liam's dad says. He looks at Liam's mom for help, but she just shrugs and points at Liam's sisters. Stephanie bursts out laughing. Not-Stephanie cough-giggles in her hand.

I like the idea of using tech to avoid unnecessary travel, but it will only work with proper prior preparation. I squint at the Murphys. "Does Person A have the appropriate equipment for a video call? How strong is their Wi-Fi?"

"Ooo, I hope Person A installed the latest operating system and program updates," Huey says. "If not, that could be bad-bad-bad."

"Oh my god," Mr. Murphy whispers.

"NINE A.M.!" Travis shouts. She beams at Liam's parents. "That's what time Person A needs to leave. No offense, but the word problem was a little light on details, so, in addition to taking time differences and wind speed into consideration, I included estimates for airplane weight, runway length, runway surface, seasonal weather, security checks, and other airport flight delays in my calculations. Astronauts-in-training are very thorough." She holds up her napkin so we can see her work.

"Nine A.M. sounds good," Liam's mom says quickly.

"Couldn't agree more," Liam's dad says. He updates the ticker—*Students: 38. Parents: 51*—and begins shoveling slices of hot pizza on our plates.

CHAPTER 24

Huey Linkmeyer

I should be feeling awesome. TravLiUeyPadgeyZezz is on a roll. We flew through Stump 'Em. We found a great table. We ate together without fighting. We decided to stop calling Travis "The Shark" and we didn't even need to vote.

So why am I starting to get stage fright already? All I can think about is having what Ritchie calls "a Liam moment" this afternoon and majorly messing up. I'm so focused on all the bad things that could happen that I completely zone out through Dr. Yee's tour-guide talk on the walk to the high school.

I don't snap out of it until I hit the auditorium-style traffic jam to get inside the science building. Middle school IDs only open doors in the middle school. Dr. Campbell's and Mr. Montanari's guest IDs don't open anything. Dr. Yee's ID works everywhere. He elbows to the front of the line to buzz us in.

Mr. Happy tells us "to proceed in an orderly fashion to the second floor where we will begin the challenge." That's what our ears hear anyways. Our feet hear, "Run! Run! Run as fast as you can up the stairs!"

Doug and I are huffing before we reach the first landing. Padgett, Liam, and Travis zip past us. Farrow's right on their heels. Hair gel globs whiz by us like missiles. One smacks a girl when her mouth is open. She gets lots of sympathy *Eews!,* even from kids who aren't on her team.

Dr. Yee decided to follow us up the stairs. We have to wait until he gets to the second floor . . . and walks to the front of where all the teams are standing . . . and checks his watch . . . and turns on his iPad before we get started. It's torture.

"You are about to begin a timed, two-part challenge that requires a lot of teamwork and trust skills that you've hopefully been building," Dr. Yee announces. "In part one, you will decide whether to turn left or right at the end of this corridor. You'll proceed to that decision tree poster"—he points down the hall at a skinny, wooden easel holding a large piece of cardboard—"and each team member will sign their name signifying that they agree with the group decision."

Dr. Campbell steps forward. "In part two, y'all will deal with the results of that choice. Turn left to make biodegradable slime in the chemistry lab. Y'all need to document your lab processes fully." She taps her watch. "Yer clock begins the minute you enter the lab. Understand?"

"How long do we have to make the slime?" JoJo from TheExcellentorators asks.

Mr. Montanari points at his watch. "Therrrty min'uts fer bu'th challenges. Watch th' clock, B-Bs. Noo wun else'll mar' tyme fer ye."

Dr. Yee points to the opposite side of the hall. "Turn right at the decision tree to face the infamous Benjamin Banneker Word Scramble in the biology lab. This challenge mixes up the letters in the names of fifteen well-known animals and plants. Be warned: many try it; few succeed. As with the chemistry contest, your clock starts the minute you enter the room. A judge will be stationed at each doorway to check you in."

"That's it?" Ritchie smirks. "Sounds easy. TheExcellentorators for the win!"

"Dr. Yee didn't mention that these are scrambles of scientific names, not common ones." Dr. Campbell smiles at Ritchie. "Y'all have fun with that."

"We are NOT doing Word Scramble," Farrow declares. "I don't like puzzles."

Dr. Yee raises his iPad like a starting flag. "Students, are you ready?"

"YES!"

Dr. Yee drops his arm. The other teams take off. They scramble, poke and prod each other to be first.

"Wait!" Doug jumps in front of us. "Listen, Dr. Yee already told us what the choices are. And Dr. Yee said the clock doesn't start until we enter a room."

"So?" Padgett looks like she's ready to trample Doug to get to the decision poster.

"So we can make our choice here," Doug explains. "Then we can walk to the decision tree and sign our names when all that"—he jumps back as somebody's shoe slides down the hall—"is done."

"Makes sense. Good idea, Doug." Padgett frowns and crosses her arms. "I'll tell you one thing, though. I'm not doing chemistry." She shakes her head. Her knee-length braid whips around like a helicopter blade. "I ride the city bus home. I'm not getting on a bus with slime in my hair."

Liam perks up. "I didn't know you rode the city bus. We pass a bunch of bus stops on the way to my house. Want a ride sometimes?" He opens the maps app on his phone. "Where do you live?"

Padgett's ears turn pink.

"Oh." Liam's face gets splotchy. "Um, if you don't want to say . . ."

"It's . . . okay. I live off Thirtieth. At the extended-stay motel." Padgett's voice sputters like an old car engine. She stares at her clogs. "I live with my grandmother. She cleans the motel. And the martial arts dojo a couple of blocks away. And sometimes she works at the UPS." She glances at Travis. "Only a few people here know." Padgett usually stares people in the eye like she's gearing up for a boxing match. But now she looks at the ceiling. Then she looks at the floor. Then she clicks her sky-blue clogs together.

"Here's what I'm thinking!" Travis pipes up. She's being extra-loud. We whip around to look at her instead of Padgett. Which—oh, I get it now—was probably the idea. "Astronauts-in-training have to be good at chemistry. But I agree with Padgett. I don't want slime in my hair." Travis grins at Padgett.

Padgett manages a shaky smile back.

"So, two votes for the Word Scramble instead of the chem lab. Word Scramble works for me too." Doug says. Now that the cluster of kids by the decision tree is thinning out, he's ready to go. He bounces on his toes. "Huey? Liam? What do you think?"

"I'm with the team, man!" Liam hoots. He's obviously feeling better.

I nod. "Works for me."

"So, I guess we're going agree on the Word Scramble then." Doug says.

We march down the hall and sign our names on the decision tree under thirteen other teams. Five teams didn't sign. They must not have been listening to the rules.

Dr. Campbell checks us in on her tablet.

Doug's mouth drops open as he looks around. He's like a little kid in a candy store. "I can't wait to start high school. We're ready *now*, right Huey?"

"Yep." I've never been in a high school classroom before. Everything's bigger. And shinier. And super official-looking. I wonder if Doug and I will be in the same classes in high school. If we're not, I wonder . . . will we still be as good of friends?

"We probably should get started," Padgett says. "Like Dr. Campbell would say, 'Time's a-wastin'.'"

Each Word Scramble workstation has a smart white-board that the judges can monitor from their tablets. Each whiteboard has fifteen scrambles followed by lines where we're supposed to write the answers.

We choose the workstation furthest away from the other teams. Padgett swivels the whiteboard so we get a close-up view of our scramble challenges.

1. PUOSLUP TOUELMRDI _____

_____

2. CIPOELIA CAUTTAIELR _____

_____

3. OHEIEOADNCIL_____

4. HTNUSONHRRYHICO NTIUAANS _____

_____

5. ILFES SCTUA _____

_____

6. UNCSA PSUUL _____

_____

7. HEARNPAT LOE _____

_____

8. USM UULSUSMC _____

_____

9. GRCOUASYOTL NUCSIUCULI _____

_____

10. IHTSRPEDAAOHE _____

_____

11. MSAUL _____

12. PURNUS ECRASPI _____

_____

13. PREAOACORLH _____

14. SCPAMLHHAERIO_____

15. CIESIRUDA_____

Doug scratches his chin. "This won't be easy."

I was hoping being able to think and write backwards would help me, but I've got nothing. I pop into a super-hero pose and stick out my neck. Still zilch.

Everybody else is guessing. I can barely hear what they're saying because my stage fright ogre starts yammering in my ears. *Everybody's watching you. What if you choose wrong? Guess who'll get blamed if there's a mistake.* My stomach feels as tight as my shoelaces.

The one thing I can do for sure is remember the rules and track our time. I check the clock. *Oh man.* "We already used five minutes!"

Doug gulps. He turns his back to the workstation. Then he leans over so he's staring at the whiteboard upside down.

"What are you doing?" Travis asks. "Is that some kind of special seventh-grade thinking thing?"

"I'm getting a different perspective." Doug's voice sounds like he's gargling. "I do it when I'm inventing. If I can't figure out something one way, I try something else. Hey!"

He whips around so fast it must make him dizzy. He jabs all over the whiteboard before settling on number eleven. "I recognize this," he hisses. We have to lean in to hear him. "It's *Malus*! You know, the scientific name for apple trees. We have two in our backyard."

Liam studies the list sideways. "This really works!" he booms. Two teams whirl around to stare. "I mean, this really works," he whispers. "Number five is *Felis catus*. That's the scientific name for cats. I love cats!"

Now that we're started, TravLiUeyPadgeyZezz flies through. We finish the Word Scramble with eight minutes to spare.

1. PUOSLUP TOUELMRDI *Populus tremuloid* (aspen tree)
2. CIPOELIA CAUTTAIELR *Poecilia reticulata* (guppy fish)
3. OHEIEOADNCIL *Chelonioidae* (sea turtle)
4. HTNUSONHRRYHICO NTIUAANS *Ornithorhynchus anatinus* (platypus)
5. ILFES SCTUA *Felis catus* (domestic cat)
6. UNCSA PSUUL *Canus lupus* (wolf)
7. HEARNPAT LOE *Panthera leo* (lion)
8. USM UULSUSMC *Mus musculus* (house mouse)
9. GRCOUASYOTL NUCSIUCULI *Oryctolagus cuniculus* (European rabbit)
10. IHTSRPEDAAOHE *Theraphosidae* (tarantula)
11. MSAUL *Malus* (apple tree)
12. PURNUS ECRASPI *Prunus persica* (peach tree)
13. PREAOACORLH *Rhopalocera* (butterfly)
14. SCPAMLHHAERIO *Selachimorpha* (shark)
15. CIESIRUDA *Sciuridae* (squirrel, chipmuck and related rodents)

Everyone but me gets at least one answer. All I do is keep time.

We're the last team to check in with Dr. Yee and the judges at the front door.

Ritchie has slime in his ears and dripping from his nostrils. "TheExcellentorators better be number one after all this." He glares at us. "If we're not, we at least better be ahead of you." He backs off when Padgett flicks her retainer.

"Glad we didn't do the chemistry challenge," Travis mutters.

Padgett gives her a fist bump. "Right!"

"Competitors, we have tabulated your results," Dr. Yee announces. "Teams MakerSpaceDemons, TheNeverLastonians, Plié'sTheThing, We♥Math, and $A^2 + B^2 = BeatU$: Paying attention to details is an important skill set. In a complex assignment, it's always helpful to have someone ensure you follow the directions. In this case, you neglected to sign the decision tree. That was an essential component of step one. As a result, you are eliminated."

"This is getting hard, y'all," Dr. Campbell says as Mr. Happy shoos the newly eliminated teams through the door. "I really appreciate the spunk yer bringing to this tourney. It's tough to see y'all go, but go you must. Team WeMayWimpOut, you failed to complete yer challenge in the allotted time. Sad to say, y'all are disqualified."

"But we came out before them!" Stoney Montgomery points at us.

"That you did. But the challenge was to watch yer time, not someone else's. Y'all completed the task in thirty-nine minutes. TravLiUeyPadgeyZezz did it in twenty-two. One of the fastest times today."

"But . . ." Stoney protests.

Dr. Campbell sticks out her arm, traffic-stop style. "Don't go turnin' over rocks, son. Ya might get snakebit. Besides, yer team also got two answers wrong. So there's that."

Mr. Montanari waves his tablet. "Aye."

"I'm sad to say that nine of the remaining teams failed to allow each person to participate in a meaningful way. As a result, you will also exit the tournament," Dr. Yee says. "Students, you've all been enthusiastic competitors. I hope you've learned some valuable lessons from this experience." He takes a quick peek at his iPad and clears his throat. "If STEAMS ends for you today, I hope I don't need to remind you that no one person is responsible for your team's fate."

His eyes are sad.

CHAPTER 25

Frederick Douglass Zezzmer

I can barely keep from dancing while Dr. Campbell, Mr. Montanari, and Mr. Happy update our punch cards.

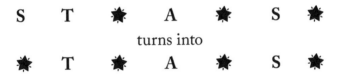

S   T   ✹   A   ✹   S   ✹

turns into

✹   T   ✹   A   ✹   S   ✹

Today is the best day ever! STEAMS is now down to three challenges and four teams. We're tied with TheExcellentorators for second place. The final score was so close that Judge Montanari said he felt like he was deciding who would get an Olympic medal. At least I think that's what he said. It's impossible to be sure.

I keep looking at the list on MeU. It's beautiful.

1. IxnayOnTheBodySpray
2. TheExcellentorators and TravLiUeyPadgeyZezz
3. TallerThanOurGrandpas

Liam's dad and Travis's dad are already waiting in the pickup lane when we get back to middle school. Padgett is about to walk to the bus stop when Mrs. Jalil pulls up and toots her horn.

"Wait—you get rides from Mrs. Jalil when you don't take the bus?" I'm pretty sure my mouth is hanging open. "I thought you were always with her because of detention."

Padgett snorts. "Yeah, I let everybody think that. It's good for my scary reputation."

Huey narrows his eyes. "Does that mean you don't have black belts in three different martial arts either?"

"Nope."

"And you didn't hack Dr. Yee's presentation?"

"Nope."

I plop beside Huey on the waiting bench after the rest of TravLiUeyPadgeyZezz leaves. "I'm beginning to think the middle school rumor mill isn't all it's cracked up to be."

"As long as the stories about the underground teacher tunnels are true, I'll be fine," Huey says. "I can't take it if

Mr. Happy beats us to homeroom alley walking the regular way." I think he's trying to sound cheerful, but his head droops. He looks like Liam after the catapult challenge.

I lob a fake Black Panther swipe at his head. We both know that it's not Mr. Happy getting to homeroom alley ahead of us that's getting him down. "You did a really good job with STEAMS today, Huey."

He shrugs and digs the heels of his shoes into the ground. "I still got stage fright."

"Yeah, I saw. But you kept helping the team anyway." At least that gets Huey to look up. "The way I see it, you'll be ready to perform at Porch View by summer break. Just keep practicing"—I pop my fists on my waist and stick out my neck—"the HueyLink superhero pose."

Huey snorts. "Right. Like he always said, 'Say cheers to fears.'" He digs in his shirt pocket. "Wanna see a card trick?"

"Sure!"

Julius picks that moment to pull into the pickup lane though. Card tricks will have to wait.

"How was your day?" he calls as we walk over.

"Amazing!" I boast. "We're number two."

Julius waggles his phone. "I've been watching the leaderboard. Good job!"

One of B-B's three million rules is that kids can only get in the car door closest to the sidewalk, so Huey climbs in the backseat first. He scoots to his regular place behind Julius. I'm getting ready to hop in after him when someone calls my name.

Julius stiffens. I wonder if something bad is coming, like that time Coach Judy charged out to complain about me filling all the basketballs with Zezzmer's Nuh-uh2Flats B-Ball Goop. (Turns out Nuh-uh gets harder than cement after a couple of hours.)

But it's not Coach Judy striding toward us. It's Pops.

I'm not sure what I'm supposed to do after our last bumper car conversation, so I just give a little wave. Pops waves too. Awkward.

"Afternoon, J.," Pops says when Julius opens the car door. "No need to get out. This won't take long."

Julius gets out anyway. It's still weird to see him stand near Pops, especially when they've both just come from work. They're the same height. About the same weight. But Julius is in his same-old-same-old pants, shirt and tie. Pops wears what Moms calls "corporate armor." Expensive suit. Silk shirt. Pricey tie. Spit-shined shoes. He gives Julius a fast up-and-down, then unloads the EZ stare.

Julius sighs. "Elliott." He doesn't do an actual eye roll, but I hear one in his voice. "How's it going?"

"Couldn't be better." Pops speaks fast. He doesn't have time for Julius, as usual. My stomach clenches, also as usual.

Julius tugs at his collar to loosen his tie. I think he's having a model volcano moment. He barely looks down when his phone starts to buzz.

"I'm taking Doug home with me today," Pops says. "He'll have dinner with us." He's not asking.

I can tell Julius wants to say no. He's got the look he always gets when he's about to say I can't do something. But CCCP means Pops has the final word when it's just the two of them.

"I called Annie a few minutes ago. That's probably her texting you now." Pops's EZ stare grin gets bigger. "Doug can sleep over if we're having too much fun after dinner to stop. He's got pajamas and a toothbrush at my house. I can drop him off at school in the morning."

Pops has it all covered. He's thought of everything. I look at Huey, who slid across the backseat to my side of the Subaru and pressed his nose against the window to watch, and shrug.

Julius takes a minute to read his texts. They're obviously from Moms. There are obviously a lot. Pops must have been convincing. Julius sighs again. "Fine." He turns to me. "FaceTime with your mom is top priority. Ten P.M. for bed is nonnegotiable. Deal?"

I blow out a breath. I know I sound like Julius when I do that. "Deal."

Julius pats my shoulder. "Then have a good time, son." Pops makes a growly sound at that. "Nate and I will keep Huey company while you're gone," Julius continues. "Call if you need anything."

Since Pops parked at the end of the pickup lane, Julius and Huey have already pulled away by the time we get to the SUV. From what he said to Julius, I expected it would just be Pops and me on the ride home, but instead, I see T.W. scowling in the front seat. *Not good.*

Pops's SUV has a Zezzmer's Auto Proofer on the dashboard. He doesn't tap it when he starts the car. I grind my teeth until my jaws ache. Is this is how Pops feels when he doesn't see his sports jersey on my wall?

Once we're on the highway and headed to his house, Pops glares at me in the rearview. "Are you ready to tell me what's going on?"

Before I can answer, T.W. leans over and throws a stack of papers in my lap. "Not funny."

I flip through the pages. "What's this?"

"Like you don't know," T.W. snaps. "Wills B. Speare? You wrote my paper about him. You said he was William Shakespeare's secret identity."

How does he know about that? My palms start sweating. My face heats up. "I didn't. I mean, I didn't on your real paper." Did DougApp accidentally send a copy of the fake paper along with the real one? *Oh no!*

"Yes, you did."

"No. I. Didn't!"

"Yes! You! Did!" T.W. yells. "I'll get an F if I turn this in."

"Then don't turn it in! I sent you a different paper for your class."

"Wait. Hold up. What are you talking about?" Pops demands. "What do you mean you sent him a paper? That's not tutoring."

T.W. and I clam up fast.

"I'm waiting!" Pops's college Orange Bowl rings tap the steering wheel impatiently. CRACK. CRACK. CRACK.

I explain as fast as I can. I have to go over how DougApp works twice. Pops and T.W. have a hard time believing I created an app that can scan for typos and send emails on its own.

I activate DougApp and turn on the audio to show them.

"Hello, Frederick Douglass Zezzmer, the world's greatest inventor," DougApp says. "How may I help?"

"What's the status on the Shakespeare paper I asked you to send to T.W.?"

"The paper was sent on Tuesday evening as directed. It was included as an attachment in an email sent to T.W.

Jackson-Zezzmer. He is listed in your contacts as Worst Step—"

"That's enough!" I yelp over the rest of T.W.'s nickname. I wave my phone at Pops and T.W. "See! It was an accident." I try to keep my voice calm. "DougApp, can you send the paper to T.W. that doesn't mention Wills B. Speare? The one that you wrote?"

There are some clicks.

Then a really long pause.

"I cannot," DougApp says. "That file does not exist. You overwrote it when you created the paper about Wills B. Speare. Per standard protocol, past versions have been deleted from all devices and from the cloud."

CHAPTER 26

T.W. Jackson-Zezzmer

f Mr. Big Brain—and yeah, Stepbruh's back to being Mr. Big Brain—thinks telling Elliott about his computer program will get him off, he's wrong. Elliott is steamed. At both of us. And none of this—okay, most of this—isn't even my fault.

"Doug, I relied on you to help T.W. so he wouldn't have to go to summer school," Elliott growls. "And T.W., I expected you to play your part. You know I don't condone cheating. Doug is supposed to be a resource for you. Like a coach."

"But I'm the oldest!" I protest.

Elliott starts breathing hard, like he's been running football plays in the sun. I feel sorry for him. When he told Ma and me that we were moving to Denver, he said this would be his time to shine. That's why he takes all those parenting classes. He wants everything to go just right. This mess with my Shakespeare paper is definitely not what he intended.

"I trusted both of you to keep your eyes on the prize," Elliott says. He's speaking super slow, like he's sounding out all his words. The AC is on, but he's sweating. His neck looks like it's starting to swell. I have a picture of him playing against the Raiders, all puffed up after he dropped a pass this one time. He kind of looks like that now. It's way scarier in real life.

He sucks in a breath. "Thanks to your bad behavior, you two might miss a great opportunity." He drums his rings against the steering wheel. "No! We are not going to let that happen. Doug, you're going to tutor T.W. through that paper. For real this time. Spend all night on it if you have to. If you don't finish, you'll stay home tomorrow and get it done."

"But what about STEAMS?" Mr. Big Brain howls. "My team is tied for second. We have a really good chance to win." He doesn't know Elliott like I do. He doesn't know when to shut up. Elliott railed about me going behind his back to switch schools the whole drive out to Banneker. Know what? I didn't say one word. By the time we picked up Mr. Big Brain, Elliott was ready to go off on something else.

"Once. Again. Doug . . . your priority is helping your brother with his paper so you *both* can do sports camp." Elliott sounds like he'd rather be tackled by a dozen linebackers than be in this car. "Please, do not make me repeat myself." He parks in the garage and herds us inside.

When we were looking for a house in Denver, Elliott said he wanted a place with an extra bedroom so Mr. Big Brain could live with us full-time. He assumed that would happen right away. It did not. The kid had a total freak-out when Elliott announced his plan. So did his mom. So did his stepdad. It was awful. Now, Elliott uses that bedroom for his den. Mr. Big Brain sleeps in a pullout in my room when he stays over.

We all pretend the den doesn't exist when we pass by it on the way to the kitchen.

Ma doesn't smile when she joins us. She manages social media and PR for all of Elliott's companies, and she usually has really long days. She looks more tired than usual though. She still gives me a hug. And she kisses Elliott's cheek. She squeezes Mr. Big Brain's shoulder. It's a nice thing to do. Stepbruh looks like he's about to bawl.

"Let's order takeout for dinner," Ma says. "I just got home from work. I know Elliott had a hard day. And you boys look like you've been through the wringer."

Mr. Big Brain trudges behind me to my room while we wait for the food. I flop on the bed. He wilts to the floor and picks at my carpet.

"I'm really sorry about the paper," he says. "I didn't mean for that to happen."

"Yeah, well, you shouldn't have made a computer write it."

He looks up long enough to glare. "You shouldn't have tried to make me write it either. Tutors aren't supposed to cheat."

"Then you should have said no the first time I asked!"

"You didn't ask me! You said, 'Get it done if you know what's good for you, Mr. Big Brain!'"

"Yeah so!"

"Yeah so!"

This is the stupidest argument in the history of arguments. "Let's just get it done, Mr. Big Brain."

"I HATE being called Mr. Big Brain!"

"Well I HATE being called the worst stepbrother in history!"

He looks shocked.

I sneer at him. "Didn't know I knew that, did you?"

"No—but I didn't start calling you the worst stepbrother in history until *you* started using my head as target practice for your football."

"Yeah so!" Dang it! I started us up again.

Stepbruh stares at me. Then he laughs a little. Me too.

"Yeah so . . . whatever," Mr. Big—Doug—says. "Show me the assignment again."

"Gimme a minute. Let me pull it up." Lucky for me, Ms. Hamilton is only old-school about bringing electronics into the classroom. My room is a disaster zone. If she handed out assignments on paper instead of emailing them to us, I'd never find it.

I slide my laptop over to Doug so he can read the assignment. He studies it for a minute, then flops on his belly and taps a few keys to open a new document.

"I could've written it myself, you know," I say. I crane my neck to the side. It's one of my secret signals in football. It tells the quarterback to call a timeout because I have something important to say. I do it now out of reflex or whatever. We're not on the field.

"I mean, I could've written it myself if I had more time," I tell Stepbruh. "And if I was interested in Shakespeare. And if I typed faster. And if I knew how to start papers and organize them. And if I didn't always get so turned around when I'm writing."

Doug blinks at me through his glasses. "Did you read everything you were supposed to?"

"Duh. That's not my problem. I read *Julius Caesar, Macbeth, Romeo and Juliet,* and a bunch of sonnets."

"Did you like them?"

"I hated the sonnets. *JC* is okay. *Macbeth* is about a really messed-up dude. *Romeo and Juliet* is wimpy."

Doug snorts. Me too.

For some reason, I want us to keep talking. It doesn't matter about what. I step over his legs and haul my stash box out of the closet. Doug's eyes go wide. When I pop off the lid and pull out a handful of books, he sighs in relief. "I always wondered what was in there."

"Bet you didn't think it would be books, huh? Who knew dumb old T.W. likes to read."

"I don't know what you like. Other than sports, I mean."

"Yeah so, now you know." I slide some of my books across the carpet. "I like sci-fi. I want to write a book of my own one day. Maybe two."

I wait for him to laugh.

But instead of laughing, he says, "Cool." He fiddles with the cover of one of my favorites. "Bradbury. I like him, too." He holds up a Butler and a Jemisin. "I haven't read these yet. They look great. Can I borrow them?"

"Seriously?"

"Yeah." He looks up and smirks. "So." Stepbruh's kind of funny. Who knew?

He hunches over my laptop and rechecks the assignment. "You know what? According to this, you can write a paper comparing Shakespeare to science fiction if you want. See?" He slides the computer toward me. I read the assignment again. Okay, I read it for the first time. Sure enough, there it is: *You may also compare and contrast the works of William Shakespeare with contemporary literature you find more appealing.*

"Totally missed that," I say. I slide the computer back. "So what are you gonna write?" He rolls his eyes. "Just kidding. What are *we* going to write?"

Doug slides the computer to me again. "Actually, I was thinking you could do this yourself."

"Nope. Can't." I slide the computer back. "I told you. My brain doesn't work like that."

"I heard you." Doug pushes my computer into the space between us. "My friend . . ." He looks like he's about to say a name and catches himself just in time. "My, uh, best friend needed help with writing, too. The learning specialist at school taught him how to plan what to write before he gets started." He yanks a pen from his pocket and grabs a scrap of paper from under a chair.

I lean over to watch him draw. I'm expecting a diagram that's as complicated as a warp core engine. Instead, he draws . . . a triangle?

I should have known this was too good to be true. "You're kidding, right?"

"No. I'm serious."

"A triangle can help me write a paper?"

"It's a pyramid." He turns it over. "An upside-down pyramid." He draws a bunch of lines so the triangle-pyramid has wide stripes.

"You use this to outline your paper. You put your main idea in the first box, the one at the base of the pyramid. Write it with power. Like, you say, *I think science fiction is better than Shakespeare because sci-fi is more interesting to kids today.*"

"Yeah so . . ." Sounds easy. "Then what?"

"Then you write a different reason for why you think science fiction is more interesting in each box except the last one." He holds my pen over the second box. "Like . . . ?"

"Uh. Like, um . . ." My voice goes up a whole octave. I don't get this nervous when I daydream ideas for the book I want to write, or when Coach says I have to make a big play. "Because it's more modern and, uh, more relevant?"

"Exactly!" Doug hoots. "Let's do more." His grin is so big you'd think he was the one who answered the question. If this is what having a little brother is like, it's cool.

We fill in all the boxes except the last one together. Guess what? It's not horrible.

"The last box is where you summarize all the other sections," Doug says. "It's kind of like saying, '*See! I proved my point. Science fiction is way better than Shakespeare. Told you, Ms. Hamilton!'"*

Huh. Writing a paper with Stepbruh is fun. I wish Elliott was in my room to see us.

Doug tries to give me the outline. I don't take it. "Sorry. We don't have time for me to write it. I'm not the world's best typer."

Doug shoves the outline in my hand. "Doesn't matter. I can install DougApp on your computer. It does dictation and it can type as fast as you talk."

"Won't help." I waggle the outline. "I can't learn to turn this into a real paper overnight."

Doug grins. "I made a special version of DougApp for my friend. It'll ask questions about the outline so you flesh it out, then it'll guide you through organizing and formatting. You really can write the paper yourself."

I wait for him to say DougApp is like training wheels on a bike. But he doesn't.

"So is DougApp going to type what I say for real, or is it going to slip in something about Wills B. Speare?"

Stepbruh rolls his eyes. "Nothing about Wills B. Speare. Trust me."

Turns out I know a lot about Shakespeare. Once Doug installs DougApp on my laptop, all I have to do is talk. Writing the paper is really easy. And comparing those old plays to books I like was fun. (I don't go near the sonnets. I bet no one but Kamiyah does either.)

By the time Doug FaceTimes with his mom, we have half the paper done.

"This is a good start," Elliott says when he checks on us later. "You're doing a good job. I'm proud of you."

"Thanks, Pops." Doug spider-crawls across my rug to grab his shoes. "Can you take me home now? It's almost nine."

Elliott shakes his head. "I decided you should spend the night. You and T.W. can stay here tomorrow and finish this paper."

Doug's face falls like an elevator. "But I have to go to school. I told you, tomorrow's the last day of STEAMS."

"And I told you, this paper is your priority."

"He doesn't have to stay, Elliott," I say. It feels weird to jump in and back up Stepbruh. But right. But still weird. "I know what to do now. I can finish the paper myself."

"That's generous of you, T.W., but Doug made a commitment. He'll see it through." Elliott turns back to Stepbruh. "You're staying here, son. I'm not discussing this. We're done."

CHAPTER 27

Huey Linkmeyer

Me: What HAPPENED?

Doug: DougApp messed up T.W.'s paper. I had to help him write a new one.

Me: I know THAT. You told me THAT 5 texts ago. I mean what happened when you called Mr. J.?

Doug: Is he mad? He sounded mad.

Me: 🔥!!! What did you tell him?

Doug: I told him everything about the paper. And that Pops doesn't care about STEAMS. And that he wants me to stay here tonight.

Me: Oof.

Doug: Yeah.

Me: Did you ask him to come get you?

Doug: Yeah. Is he coming?

Me: 🚀!!! I'm hanging with Mr. Cohen while he's gone.
Me: Did you tell him anything else?
Doug: That Pops won't listen to me. That I want to come home.

CHAPTER 28

Julius Jordan

It's a good thing I do yoga. It keeps me calm. Helps me breathe. Still, I can only imagine what I look like when I ring the doorbell at Elliott's house to pick up Doug.

I called Annie before I left. I haven't heard her this angry since Elliott announced he wanted Doug to live in his new house—two days after he moved back to Denver.

Annie called Elliott while I was driving. Elliott looks like he's been on the wrong side of a lawn mower when he answers the door.

Patrice doesn't look happy, either. She knows all the details now.

"Hello, Julius," she says with a nod. She glares at Elliott. "I'll wait for you in the kitchen. We still have a lot to discuss."

"Doug!" Elliott aims his shout toward the stairs. Doug barrels down a few seconds later, lugging his backpack.

He's obviously ready to leave. T.W. follows halfway. He stays put when Doug trots over to stand by me. I drape an arm across his shoulders.

"Annie was all fired up when she called, so let's be clear about one thing, J." Elliott says. "I didn't know the boys had a scheme for Doug—or DougApp, or whatever it is—to write T.W.'s paper. Or that they've done this kind of thing before. I explained that to Annie. And Patrice. Tried to anyway . . ." He rubs his temples. "Man . . ."

He looks at Doug. "Help me out here. Did I ever ask you to cheat?"

"No."

"See!" Elliott raises his hands and looks around as if everything's resolved. As if everything's over. "I obviously should've kept a closer eye on the boys. I own that."

One thing I've learned from all my years with Doug is that sometimes the best thing you can do is just listen. Sooner or later, people tell you what they really want.

Elliott folds his arms. He gives me the EZ stare. Yeah—I looked it up. It's supposed to be intimidating. Obviously Elliott didn't grow up in foster care in Brooklyn. *That* is intimidating.

"Glad we got that settled," Elliott says. "I'm feeling much better." He rocks back on his heels. "There's still the matter of the paper, though."

There it is.

Doug stiffens under my arm.

"T.W. needs to turn it in by Friday. And there was a commitment to help with tutoring," Elliott says. "Annie, Patrice, and the boys have this idea about T.W. writing the paper on his own."

I jump in. "That's a good idea." Doug relaxes beside me. "Like Annie told you, Doug will be in school all day tomorrow. But I'm sure he'll have time in the evening to check the paper for typos. After you review it yourself, of course."

Doug looks up at me. "Tomorrow night? But Huey and I are going to . . ."

"New plan. You're grounded."

"But . . ."

"Grounded with no unsupervised tech. And that's just the start of your punishment, trust me."

"Okaaaay." Doug sighs. He meets Elliott's eyes. "I'm sorry I got you in trouble, Pops."

"Me too," Elliott says. He winces as something bangs in the kitchen. "I have a feeling you're not the only one who's going on punishment, little man."

Once we get home, I give Doug a few minutes to commiserate with Huey before calling him downstairs to FaceTime with Annie at the kitchen table. She doesn't waste any time.

"What were you thinking, Doug? Why on earth would you believe it was okay to help T.W. cheat?"

Doug wipes a drop of sweat from his brow. "We only did it once, Moms. I felt awful. That's why I didn't cheat this time. Not technically anyway. I used DougApp."

Annie holds up a warning finger. She's still wearing her power makeup. She leans in close to her camera. "Do. Not. Go. There."

Doug gulps. "I mean . . . okay. It's a gray area." Annie arches an eyebrow. Doug powers on. "You said I had to get Pops to agree on what I want to do this summer. He said the only way he'll consider letting me do GadgetCon is if T.W. gets a good grade on his paper. And I have to do GadgetCon."

"You mean you *want* to do GadgetCon."

"No. I HAVE to."

Annie looks at me. I shrug. No clue.

"Why?" I ask.

"Because!" Doug slaps both palms on the table. "If I go to GadgetCon, it means Pops decided I don't have to do sports camp. And if Pops decides I don't have to do camp, that means he finally realizes that inventing is just as important as sports. And if Pops decides inventing matters, he'll *finally* stop trying to make me give up everything I like and be just like him." He drags an arm across his nose. "Sometimes he makes me so mad, Moms!"

I've been a stepfather long enough to have seen Doug upset plenty of times. But this—this is different. Seeing Doug so miserable hits me like a punch to the stomach.

"I want to be an inventor more than anything," Doug whispers. "I want to make gadgets that solve problems and make people happy." He pushes his glasses up and pretends not to notice they slide down again because his nose is damp with tears. "I know I can."

I look at Annie. Her eyes are wide.

"Doug, sweetie. I'm sorry this has been so hard on you." She wipes away tears. "There are a few things you should know. First, Julius and I are behind you a thousand percent with whatever you want to do with your life. Inventing. Sports. Something else entirely." She sighs. Suddenly, she looks exhausted. "Second, your father's learning. Hands-on parenting . . . that's new to him. He may think he has all the answers, but he doesn't. Give him time."

"So you'll talk to Pops?"

"Oh, honey, of course . . ." Annie gives me a "help please" look. I tag in to deliver the bad news.

"But . . . that doesn't mean you aren't in trouble. You are going to be grounded and on all types of other punishment for a long, long time. GadgetCon may be a wonderful, fun, exciting event, Doug, but it's optional. It's not tied to any of your grades, or to the advanced STEM programs you want to attend in a few years."

Doug looks at me. "Even if Dr. Yee invites me, you're not going to let me go this summer, are you?"

"Correct." *Thump!* Doug's head drops face down on the table. I repeat the decision, just so we're clear. "Even if Dr. Yee invites you, you're not going. Understand?"

"Yesss," Doug moans. He's speaking into the wood. His voice is muffled. "Does this mean I have to do sports camp?"

"Not unless you want to," Annie says, tagging back in. "I'll help your father understand that. But there is one more thing."

Doug rolls his head. A weary eyeball peeps up at the screen. "I can't take any more, Moms." I try not to laugh.

Annie steeples her hands in front of her mouth. Her eyes crinkle. She's trying not to laugh either.

"I thought working together to figure out your summer plans would be a good way for you and your father to connect," she says after a minute. "I thought the stakes were low enough that nothing major would go wrong. Clearly, that was a mistake." Annie puts her stern face back on. "What happened this week is a clear example of why you and Elliott have to learn to talk with each other."

"But he doesn't listen, Moms."

"Funny. He says the same thing about you."

"All he cares about is sports."

"Funny. He says all you care about is inventing."

"So you're on his side!" Doug whines.

Annie raises both eyebrows this time. "I'm on your side, Doug. I'm always on your side. Which is why I'll tell you the same thing I told your father. Sooner or later, the two of you have to talk about what's really bothering you. For the record, it's not sports."

"But . . ."

Annie looks at me. I get that punch in the stomach feeling again—but it's nerves this time. I know what she's about to say. "And it's not inventing."

Instead of going straight to school the next morning, we stop at the airport to pick up Annie. She was always planning to fly back on Friday to surprise Doug with a "Yay! You made it through STEAMS" celebration, but she cut her trip short after the T.W. paper debacle. Her phone's been buzzing nonstop since she got in the car. She ignores it.

I glance in the rearview and catch Huey using American Sign Language to say, *Your mom really turned down the promotion?* in the backseat. Doug's hands fly. He's signing the short version of the story. Annie said no to the promotion. She was always leaning in that direction, but something about what happened with Doug and Elliott made her decide to speak her mind.

She also gave her notice. An hour later, so did three of the top people on her team. They won't stay without her.

Annie's going to start her own business. Fantastiske Babywear wants to be her first client as soon as she's ready. Her old company is desperate to keep her. Her boss has been calling and texting since she landed at the airport.

She said she's been thinking about it for a long time, Doug signs to Huey. *But since she's happy about it, maybe she'll change her mind and go easy on my punishment.*

I laugh-cough in my hand. Little do they know, Annie and I understand everything they're saying. Huey's not the only one his stepfather taught to sign.

I laugh-cough again. Annie glances at me curiously. We have a few other tricks, too. I drum my fingers on the steering wheel to explain.

Morse code—Parent Version. Ha!

Annie giggles and taps a reply on the armrest. It's so funny I can't help but laugh out loud.

I start to drumbeat an answer when Doug leans forward and pokes his head in the space between the driver and front passenger seats.

"Hey. What are you guys doing up there?"

Should we tell him? Annie taps while softly humming one of my favorite show tunes as a cover.

No way, I drum back. *Not while we have an advantage.*

"Moms?" Doug looks at Annie. "Julius?" Doug looks at me. "Are you up to something?"

"Just chillin'." I flip on the radio. Even though Doug-gApp is temporarily disabled, the radio is still set to Da Broadway Boyz.

Doug eyeballs me skeptically.

"Seriously?" I ask. "Doug, you're looking right at us. What could we possibly be doing?"

CHAPTER 29

Dr. Yee

I t's the last day of the competition. Are you excited?" my friend Destiny asks. We're walking along a path that leads to the no-tackle football field where the final challenges will take place. It's marked with pavers for Ronald McNair, Judith Resnik, Mae Jemison, and Sally Ride.

"Relieved, to be honest," I say. "I don't think I could take much more."

Students point and whisper "The DOM! It's The DOM!" as we pass, but they keep a respectful distance. For now.

"Just between us, I was incredibly nervous about this STEAMS competition," I admit. "I wanted the kids to discover the value of working together and picking themselves up if they fail, but it was scary. For them. For the staff and the teachers. For me. Maybe especially for me.

I don't know if you remember from middle school, but I don't like to mess up."

"Oh, I remember." Destiny jumps when a miniature drone the size of a hummingbird buzzes her ear.

I pluck it out of the air, pull out the batteries, and stick it in my pocket. Whoever was flying it should know the rule about unsanctioned motorized objects is there for a reason.

"Do you think we ever stop being who we were in middle school?" I ask.

"You mean the wide-eyed kids who thought they could handle anything? I hope not!" A second drone hums by. This time Destiny grabs it. Before she removes the batteries, she wags her finger in front of the camera signaling the end of reconnaissance missions.

"Middle school is painful in a lot of ways," she says. "Everything's changing. Some of the friendships you hope will last forever, don't." She loops an arm through mine. "And some friendships you didn't expect to make, turn out to be awesome."

The bleachers are packed when we arrive on the sports field. They're full of grumpy students who've been disqualified, exhausted teachers, and a very relieved Mrs. Jalil. Even though the students aren't happy to be on the sidelines, they can't help but gawk at the impressive five-station obstacle course we've set up for the sports tournament. It has four climbing walls, one for each team; four low balance beams, each of which spans a small mud pool; four sets of climbing bars; four curved walls that look like waves; and four well-spaced SUV tires, one for each team to flip twice.

Four doorjambs with locked wooden doors stand in a different part of the field waiting for the technology competition.

I wait for Destiny to find a seat on the bleachers. Then I scan the crowd. A lot of cranky faces stare back. It's unsettling. I imagine doing Destiny's superhero pose to settle my nerves.

"Greetings, Benjamin Banneker community," I proclaim. "Welcome to the final day of the inaugural STEAMS competition! For the past few days, you've undertaken tests that were strange, confusing, and—let's admit it—downright weird. Why? Because in the midst of those wacky events, you also learned to pivot, analyze, adapt, prioritize, and work together to solve problems you've never seen before. In the real world, the people who can do that are the ones who will solve our greatest physical, environmental, and social challenges. Hopefully, you've had fun competing, you're excited about the final contests, and you're looking forward to our all-day celebration tomorrow."

I hoist my trusty iPad in the air. "Today, we'll crown our victorious team. Give it up! Give it up!" I just love saying that. I never got to say it in middle school. "But first, we need to complete the final three challenges: technology, arts, and sports. We will begin with technology."

I direct the remaining four teams to each stand in front of one of the locked doors. The kids would be speechless if they knew Mr. Happy built the doorframes and installed the doors, doorknobs, and locks. According to the rumor mill, he has the energy of a rock. Little do the kids know that Mr. Happy is a master carpenter. He's also a long-time marathoner who takes fiendish delight in beating them to homeroom every day.

My nerves must show. Somebody gives an encouraging whoop. I have to smile. I recognize the voice. It belongs to one of the kindest kids—and the only amateur ventriloquist—at our school. "Thank you, Ramón!"

"Aw, man. C'mon, Dr. Yee!"

"Everybody, give it up for Ramón!" I feel better now. "Remaining competitors, once the challenge starts, run as a team to the wooden door in front of you. The doors are secured with locks. The code to open the lock is typed on paper located in a box in front of each door. One of the lines of code has an error. A description of the error is in red. Using your coding skills, find and correct the mistake, then present your solution to Mr. Montanari.

If your solution is correct, he will unlock the door. This will complete the technology portion of our challenge. Remember, realizing that a problem exists is not the same as discovering where and why it occurs and taking action. That's true in coding, and it's true in life. I encourage you to keep Benjamin Banneker values in mind during this challenge: Respect, Kindness, Wisdom, Community, Heart."

TheExcellentorators look powerful. Farrow has them sing their team song to get motivated. LaVontay does ballet stretches. JoJo gets into a racing position. Ritchie sneers. Pixie dunks an invisible basketball.

TallerThanOurGrandpas bounce on their toes. But they don't look at each other. I heard they're not getting along anymore.

Three members of IxnayOnTheBodySpray are arts peeps. They're focused on artistic interpretation. They're teaching their teammates some sort of jazz dance to get pumped up.

It's TravLiUeyPadgeyZezz who have me worried. Douglass in particular. His mother called me this morning and explained why this competition meant so much to him. Now that there's no chance of going to Gadget-Con this summer, does he even care about his team anymore?

CHAPTER 30

Frederick Douglass Zezzmer

'm so in it to win it with my team!

At first, I wasn't sure how I'd feel about finishing the competition. Then I remembered Dr. Yee telling the first teams who were disqualified to use failures to get better. If that advice is good enough for kids who thought calling themselves RMomsWillBeMadIfWeLose was a smart idea, it's good enough for me.

When Dr. Yee tells us it's time to start the technology contest, all the teams have a different way of entering the sports field.

TheExcellentorators march in, one after another, like an Olympic gymnastics team. They take Door #4.

We do a messy, laughy huddle-walk/group-run. It turns out, Travis squeals when she's excited. And she's squealing a lot this morning! I have to keep reminding myself that she's just a little kid.

We choose Door #3 because three was Liam's number when he was on B-B's no-tackle football team. He rode the bench the whole season, but the team still did okay, all things considered. They only had two games. Both ended in a draw—which is why Liam figures the number three is lucky.

"This is going to be a really weird competition," Padgett whispers. The doors look like displays at a hardware store. A box with a stack of paper sits in front of each one like Dr. Yee said, but there're no computers, no screens, nothing techy. "It's an open-air challenge," she warns. "Keep your voices low while we're working so nobody hears what we say."

She flicks her retainer at Ritchie. He's been scrutinizing us closely, scowling. But she smiles and waves at the other TheExcellentorators. Farrow's the first to wave back. His hair is shellacked flat today. I have no idea why until he points to his head and shouts, "I'm using my homemade, aerodynamics-enhancing hair gel. It cuts wind drag so I can run faster in the sports challenge. I use it in track all the time." He gives me a thumbs-up. "I invent too, Zezz!"

Who knew?

IxnayOnTheBodySpray take Door #2. They do some kind of twisty, squirmy dance thing into the competition area. When they finish, they bow for applause. We're good humans. We clap. Sometimes, being good humans is all you can do.

TallerThanOurGrandpas stomp to Door #1.

"They're mad-mad-mad," Huey whispers. "I heard three of them had a party last night and they didn't invite the other two. The inviters got in an argument at the party, so they're fighting. The kids who weren't invited aren't talking to the inviters, and they're angry at each other, too. I don't know why."

Liam looks up from stuffing his Thor hair under a baseball cap that has MURPHY5 (for the fifth member of his family) stitched on the front. "How do you even know all this stuff?"

Huey shrugs. "The rumor mill. It's loaded with details. Like, did you know Mr. Happy only takes three hundred steps on weekends? He barely moves."

Dr. Yee cups his hands to make a human megaphone. "Competitors, you may now start the technology competition," he yells. "You will have thirty minutes. Remember to signal Mr. Montanari when you have a solution. Dr. Campbell will keep time."

Good news: Even though the packet of code is five pages long, it's written in, like, fourteen-point type. It's easy to read, and there aren't that many lines of text to review.

Bad news: Liam stares at it like it's hieroglyphics. Huey looks back at the bleachers, pops into a HueyLink pose, and turns his back on the crowd . . . and on the code.

Travis moves away, too. "Astronauts-in-training obviously know how to code. But we also know how to step back when there are other people on the team who do it better." She juts her chin at me and Padgett. No pressure.

There's no math in our code, so we don't have to worry about a computer trying to calculate something that can't be calculated.

"No obvious syntax errors," Padgett says. "No missed brackets or bad punctuation."

I point to four lines of red letters. "These don't help much. They tell us when the error occurred, but they don't tell us why."

"I wish we had someone to talk to about this. You know, somebody who had a problem like this before and can tell us how they solved it." Padgett sticks her nose right on the paper like that might help. "Their solution might not work for us exactly, but it would be a great place to start."

"Yeah . . . but I can't help thinking that we were given a clue. I'm just not sure where." I shift into inventing mode. I design a door-opening device in my head. Then I imagine all of the software I'd need to get the door to open and close. Then I go back to scanning the code for this challenge one row at a time. It's slow work.

"Fifteen minutes!" Dr. Campbell calls.

"How are we supposed to solve this?" Ritchie yells from Door #4. "It's so unfair!"

TallerThanOurGrandpas are shouting. I hear rustling paper. It sounds like someone threw all their pages in the air. But I don't stop proofing.

"Competitors, I have an announcement," Dr. Yee calls. "Team TallerThanOurGrandpas has quit the competition due to creative differences."

Padgett snorts. "That's one way to say it."

Liam tries reading the code sideways. It worked for the science challenge. "Aw man," he groans. "I thought at least there'd be a clue or something."

"Me too." Padgett mutters. She taps her hands against her head like she's playing the drums. "But all Dr. Yee said was to keep Benjamin Banneker values in mind during the challenge. What are we supposed to do with that?"

"Time for a word from our sponsor!" Ritchie hollers. "Attention, TheExcellentorators: Everybody who's not coding sing with me."

Ex-cel-lent.
Ex-cel-lent.
Ex-cel-len-tor-a-tors.
We're supersmart.
We're also strong.
We're genius alligators.

"Make it stop already," one of the IxnayOnThe-BodySprayers moans. "I can't hear that song again. I value my ears!"

Oh. My. God. My brain goes cold. "That's it!"

Padgett slaps a hand over my mouth. "Shh! It's a contest, remember? We're still competing."

"But—"

"WHIS-per."

Travis, Huey and Liam rush over. Liam pulls us into a five-kid huddle. We hunch over the code. "Listen." I keep my voice low. "Dr. Yee told us to remember the B-B values, right?"

"Yes. Respect, Kindness, Wisdom, Community, Heart," Travis mutters.

"Yeah so, none of the actual values are in the code, but . . ."

"The word *values* is." Padgett gets it.

"Right!" I jab the paper. "Up here, the code says, Values = OPEN. But down here, where the code needs to execute the command, it says Values = OPNE."

"It's a typo!" Travis hisses. "He bugged the code with a simple typo."

"Yeah. It only takes one bad word to ruin code." This is almost too easy. We break formation and I scribble our correction on the paper. "We're done!" I wave at the judges.

"NO WAAAAAAAY!" Ritchie screams.

Mr. Montanari walks over and studies my notes carefully. "Ye thin' ye solved this, di' ye, Douglass?"

"It wasn't just me. We all solved it." I pat my Afro. Sharing credit feels way better than I thought it would. I just hope everybody's willing to share the blame if I'm wrong.

"Tha' remains ta be seen." Up close, Mr. Montanari smells like peppermint Lifesavers and cinnamon rolls. Who knew the judges got snacks? Great. We're right in the middle of a competition and I'm starting to get hungry.

Mr. Montanari grins and flips his beard over one shoulder. I'll be he knows exactly what I'm thinking. He digs in his pocket and pulls out a key ring full of keys. Each key has a little tag.

"If yer solution matches th' tag on th' key fer ye dur nu'ber, I'll open the dur fer ye. If it doesn', I'll pu' th' wrong key in th' dur an' ye'll star' agin."

He studies my solution again, then walks s-l-o-w-l-y to the door. He turns his back so we can't see which key he puts in the lock. Then he steps to the side and turns the knob even more s-l-o-o-o-w-l-y than before.

"Tea' TravinBs', er, LeeLaLu', er, ooo me, I ca'nuh say it. Ye, ye wee B-Bs 'ere befor' me . . . Ye ha' completed the task!"

CHAPTER 31

Padgett Babineaux

From: babineauxp
To: grams

Hi Grammy,

How are you feeling? Good, I hope. This is your 1 P.M. reminder to take your afternoon blood pressure pill. Did you do it already?

I have so much to tell you! Not just about STEAMS, but other stuff, too.

1. (This *is* about STEAMS) TravLiUeyPadgey-Zezz won the technology competition!! We're number one! (Mrs. Jalil's going to take a picture of the leaderboard and send it to your phone.)

2. Our punch cards look like this now:

✴ T ✴ A ✴ S ✴

just got changed to

✴ ✴ ✴ A ✴ S ✴

3. Liam Murphy's mom is going to call you. Her
   name is Olivia. (Don't worry. I call her
   Mrs. Murphy but she said you should call her
   Olivia. I'm just telling you so you'll know who
   she is.) Anyway, Liam said she said it would be
   easy for them to give me a ride to school in the
   mornings. I won't have to take the city bus
   anymore!

I have to go now! We're starting the next to last
challenge in a few minutes. Go, TravLiUeyPadgeyZezz,
Go!

Wish us luck!!!!

P.

CHAPTER 32

Frederick Douglass Zezzmer

L unch is awesome. It's vegan tacos, salad, cherry pie, and no Stump 'Em.

All the TravLiUeyPadgeyZezzers stop eating after two servings because the next challenge is sports. Even TheExcellentorators take it slow. All of them except Ritchie, that is. He has five helpings of everything. He probably has a cast-iron stomach from all the sportster stuff he does.

Once we go back to the playing field, Dr. Yee gives the three remaining teams—TheExcellentorators, IxnayOnTheBodySpray, and TravLiUeyPadgeyZezz—time to check out the obstacle course before we decide who's going to do what.

Travis takes the tire flip.

"Are you sure?" Liam makes a square with his fingers. He holds them up like he's measuring the tire. "It's almost as big as you."

"I can do it. Astronauts-in-training have to be prepared to exert themselves at a moment's notice. Besides, like I told Doug and Huey when STEAMS started, I'm freakishly strong for my size."

"Then I'll do the balance beam," Padgett offers. She twists her hair into a tight spiral and wraps it around her head. She holds it place with a huge, orange binder clip. It's a . . . look. No judgment. "There wasn't a bench at my bus stop for the longest time," Padgett continues. "I used to hop one-footed across rocks while I waited. It was fun. Kind of. Thanks to that, I have excellent balance."

"That leaves the climbing wall, the curved wall, and the monkey bars," I say. I look at Liam and Huey. "This is like PE 2.0. I already know I suck. Which one do you guys want?"

"I kind of remember doing the monkey bars in lower school," Huey says. "I can try those."

"And I'll take the curved wall," Liam says. "I'm pretty sure I can do it if I pretend I'm a cat."

"That leaves me with the climbing wall," I say. I push up my glasses and study the apparatus skeptically. I can already feel my hands sweating. Seriously. Who thinks these things up? "What are the rules again? Grab those little knobby things to go up?"

"Yes," Travis says. "But the good news is there's a slide on the back so you don't have to work hard to get down.

When we line up to start, I'm in the second lane, smack in the middle. Farrow's in lane one. Lelu Keenan from IxnayOnTheBodySpray is in lane 3. That's when I realize one of my shoelaces is untied.

Farrow leaves the rest of us in the dust when Dr. Yee shouts, "Go!" No lie. Lelu is taking a selfie. I'm tying my shoes.

I'll have to look at the video later to be sure, but I think the climbing wall is kind of a disaster. Farrow's already halfway down the slide by the time I get my hand on the second knobby thing. Then, when I get to the top, I can't figure out which leg to throw over so I can slide down.

I'm about to go into inventor mode to design a solution when I hear Travis yelling, "It's not a STEM problem, Doug. Just go!"

So I do.

Except, instead of sliding down on my butt like I'm supposed to, I get turned around sideways. I roll down like a log. When I land at the bottom, I'm so dizzy I wander in circles for what feels like forever before I stagger to the balance beam to do the handoff.

Padgett wasn't kidding about having great balance. She flies across the beam. Because of the lead Farrow had, JoJo Davies must've thought she had enough time to take a selfie like Lelu. But Padgett shows her. TheExcellentorators, IxnayOnTheBodySpray and TravLiUeyPadgeyZezz finish almost neck and neck.

Huey, Pixie and Scotty Roosevelt from IxnayOnTheBodySpray compete on the monkey bars. Now that we're finished, Padgett and I start chanting to give Huey encouragement. "Go, Huey!"

It doesn't help. Pixie scoots across like she's being propelled by jet fuel. She leaves Huey and Scotty way behind. That's totally unfair because, in spite of his team name, Scotty wears A LOT of body spray. And he's really sweating. I can almost see the steam cloud of triple action, extra power, cedar-scented body spray that forms over the monkey bars.

I sympathy-gag with Huey. He should get bonus points for ending his event in a tie.

"That was so awful," he wheezes as we run to the curved wall to tap in Liam. "I think my lungs literally shut down."

Bartley Eesuola from Ixnay zips up and over the curved wall without looking back. Ritchie's had three failed attempts by the time Liam sprints up. He squeaks out a tired, "Lookie here. It's the 'I got it! I got! Oops—I dropped it!' man." Then he dashes away to try the wall again.

Only two words for that attempt. Epic. Miss.

"What are you doing?" Farrow bellows as Ritchie lies gasping on the ground. The other TheExccllentorators shout, "Get up!"

"We need to encourage Liam," I tell Huey and Padgett. "What should we say?"

"I know," Huey says. *"Be a cat! Be a cat! Be a cat-cat-cat!"*

Padgett and I join in. It's kind of a song. Not an on-key song. But still a song.

Liam hears us. He rubs his hand and lines up with the middle of his curved wall. He arches his back like a cat. Then, he closes his eyes.

Ritchie's still on the ground when Liam runs by him.

He's on the ground when Liam reaches the part where the wall starts to curve and he'll have to reach up to grab the edge if he doesn't want to fall.

He's on the ground when Liam grabs the edge and hangs on, his legs pumping.

And he's still on the ground when Liam pulls himself up and over and slides down the wall to complete the station.

Liam taps in Travis. Then he, Padgett, Huey, and I wait to see if the smallest girl in middle school can really flip a tire. Zenobia Murray, an eighth grade IxnayOnThe-BodySprayer, is having a really hard time.

Travis rubs her hands together like Liam did. I think she looks nervous. Kind of like she did when she wandered the aisles in assembly, looking for a place to sit.

"You've got this!" I yell. Padgett, Huey, Liam, and I start chanting, "Go, Travis! Go, Travis! Go, Travis!"

Then all the kids and teachers in the stands start chanting. "Go, Travis! You've got this, Travis! Go-go-go!!" No one calls her The Shark.

Farrow and LaVontay are still waiting for Ritchie to make it over the wall. But they're also watching our tire flip attempt from TheExcellentorators' lane. Their mouths are moving. I can't believe it. They're chanting "Go, Travis!" too.

It's like everybody in the school—well, everybody except Ritchie—wants Travis to succeed.

All the chanting sounds awesome. I wonder if this is the first time Travis has had so many people want her to soar. She starts squealing and doing little hops from foot to foot. I'll bet she's feeling the way I feel whenever people cheer for one of my inventions.

Travis rubs her hands once more.

She looks at me.

She nods.

"I've got this," she says.

And then she flips her tire two times without even breaking a sweat.

CHAPTER 33

Travis Elizabeth Cod

I AM
an
astronaut–
in-training.

I WILL BE
the first person
to walk
on
Mars.

But . . .

I AM also
TravLi

Uey
Padgey
Zezz.

I AM NOT
a shark or a
cactus
or a porcupine
or any of the
spiky things
people used to call me.

Unless
I need to show them
I can be spiky,
if I have to,
I guess.

I WILL
tell Daddy
about winning STEAMS
at dinner
because I'm sure
we will
win.

In my mind,
I will tell Mommy,
too.

My friend
(it's so weird to say that)
but my friend
Padgett says
it's okay to talk to people
who aren't here
anymore.

She says
she sometimes
talks
to her parents,
too.

When I apply to Astronaut Camp
again
for the summer,
this is what I'll tell them
about STEAMS.

I'll say,
I AM STILL

an
astronaut–
in-training.

I WILL STILL
be
the first person
to walk
on
Mars.

But now,
I have friends
to sit with
at lunchtime.

Now,
I know
how to be
on a team.

My friends,
and my dad,
—and Mommy,
who's always watching me

from somewhere—
will be happy when
I become an astronaut
and fly away
to the stars.

CHAPTER 34

Frederick Douglass Zezzmer

*O**kay. All right.*

We beat IxnayOnTheBodySpray in the sports challenge, but just barely. For the record, I own it. A turtle could have passed me on the climbing wall. Maybe a little bit of sports this summer wouldn't be such a bad thing.

"Check it out!"

Huey waves his punch card at me.

"I got yours, too." He sails my card at me like a Frisbee. Amazingly, I catch it. Ha! What was I thinking?

I've got sportster skills. I don't need summer sports camp!

"We will now begin the final challenge," Dr. Yee proclaims. "Team TheExcellentorators and Team TravLiUeyPadgeyZezz, make your way to the field." He studies us when we get to the open space in front of the bleachers.

TravLiUeyPadgeyZezz and TheExcellentorators (except for Ritchie) are clumped together. Liam and LaVontay speed-finish a game of rock-paper-scissors. JoJo and Travis gossip about rocket trajectories. Huey and I hunker over our punch cards. Padgett and Farrow talk about physics. And smile. A lot. Who knew physics was so smiley? Not the rest of us, that's for sure.

"This last contest is designed to remind you that everything is connected," Dr. Yee says. "There's art in science, and math, and engineering, and technology. And you don't have to look too hard to find an essence of STEM in the arts." He fake plays a piano. He does a little dance of some kind. He rocks an air guitar. Surprise. He's kind of fun for a principal.

"So anyway," Dr. Yee pants when he finishes playing every instrument imaginable, "your task for the STEAMS finale is to create an arts presentation that clearly incorporates some aspect of STEM. You can create anything you want as long as you finish in fifteen minutes." He gets serious. "Team TravLiUeyPadgeyZezz and Team

TheExcellentorators, we calculated all the points from the previous competitions. You enter this contest tied. Whoever wins this final challenge will be the official STEAMS champion!"

He tosses a coin. Ritchie calls "Heads!" before anyone else can say a word.

It's tails. TheExcellentorators have to go first. Ha!

"What are we going to do?" I scan the TravLiUey-PadgeyZezz huddle. Clearly, we're all in shock. Fifteen minutes is no time.

I nod at the deck of magic cards in Huey's pocket. He catches my eye and shakes his head hard.

"Does anybody dance?" Travis asks. She glances at me, then looks away fast. "Dance well, I mean."

Fair enough. I fell off the stage tap-dancing during the last mandatory participation talent show. It was a moment.

"If we had a little more time, I'd write a short story." Liam's ears turn pink. "I'm into fanfic."

"I can juggle," Padgett volunteers. "But only socks. And only two at a time. And only when they first come out the dryer and are warm. And only green socks for some reason, so . . ."

"I got it!" Huey says. He won't meet my eyes. "We can do a musical. Every time I'm in the car with Doug's dad . . . uh, with Mr. J. . . . . he's playing show tunes on the radio. We can change the words to a song everybody knows."

Really? Now he has an idea. And it's this? I aim my best EZ stare impression at Huey. He knows about mondegreen. There's no way I'll remember the words.

Huey dashes over and pulls me out of earshot of the rest of the team. "I've been thinking about it," Huey says quickly. "Mondegreen isn't like stage fright. You don't have an imaginary ogre telling you everything that can go wrong." He pats my shoulder Julius-style. "You can do this. As long as you don't get distracted, you'll be fine."

"No way!" But that's all I get out before we get swarmed by the rest of TravLiUeyPadgeyZezz.

"Ooo, a musical," Travis yelps. "I love musicals. I used to see them all the time with my mom."

"I gave a lot of thought to being an arts peep," Padgett says solemnly. "Maybe I still will. After I win the Nobel Prize, of course."

"I'm really loud but not a great singer," Liam pronounces. He puffs out his chest. "I learned to project sitting on the bench during football season. Listen." He throws back his head and bellows, "Yaaaaaaaah!"

He's loud all right. I pound my ears to stop the ringing. If we had more time to plan—and maybe if I didn't care what the rest of TravLiUeyPadgeyZezz wanted—I could still flat-out say no. But that's not happening.

Besides, like Huey said, I'll be fine.

Fifteen minutes later, TheExcellentorators march to the middle of the sports field. They look great. Except for Ritchie. His face is as sweaty as my armpits. And, he looks a little green.

Farrow does a deep bow. He glances down. The notes scrawled on the backs of his hands are visible even from the sidelines. *Such a great idea!* Why didn't we think of that?

"Greetings, Benjamin Banneker community." Farrow sounds like Dr. Yee. "Prepare to be dazzled. Prepare to be shocked. For one afternoon only, TheExcellentorators will present an original interpretive dance called 'L'Ode to Geometry: A Tribute to Shapes.' Envisioned and choreographed by LaVontay. Starring LaVontay, Ritchie, JoJo, Pixie, and me, Farrow McLeod."

He glances down again. "Wave your arms!" he blares. *Oops!* He just read a stage direction. His face blazes red.

"It's okay!" Padgett yells. "Keep going!"

Farrow gulps. "First, behold the many faces of the parallelogram. One-two-three-GO!"

The other TheExcellentorators spin and prance into position. They grab hands and form a square. JoJo's on the top. Ritchie's the base. LaVontay and Pixie are the sides.

"As you can see, the common square is a parallelogram." Farrow sneaks a quick look at his hand. "Changing the, um, angles doesn't matter as long as the sides remain equal. One-two-three-GO!"

Pixie leans left. LaVontay leans right. Their arms are still parallel, even when two sides of their geometric shape slant.

TheExcellentorators form a circle, an oval, and a rhombus. I have to admit, they look pretty good.

"Next, we will undertake the death-defying contortion called the trapezoid," Farrow announces. He stares at his hand. He's straight-up reading his notes now. "As you know, trapezoids have only one set of parallel lines. Silence please as my team contemplates their plan. They will lie on the ground for this move. One-two-three-GO!"

LaVontay pirouettes to his spot. JoJo and Pixie turn somersaults to reach theirs. Ritchie tries to spin like a figure skater. He has to stop, drop, and crawl to position when he gets dizzy.

"I think I'm going to hurl," he gasps.

JoJo covers her face with her hands. "Eeew! Hold it in!"

"Don't get sick," LaVontay warns. His eyes narrow into slits. He holds up a warning finger. He looks like he swallowed a thundercloud. "You DO NOT want to see what happens if you puke on my shoes."

"It helps if you pinch your nose," Pixie suggests. "That's what I do. Just don't hold your breath because when you open your mouth, vomit will spray *every*where. Voice of experience. Trust me."

They complete the trapezoid at superfast speed.

"For our last act, we will attempt the treacherous right triangle." Farrow says. "It's notable for its, um . . . its, uh . . ." He's major stress-sweating now. He drags his hand through his hair. It comes back slick with goo.

"Oh no." Padgett squeezes her eyes shut.

Thanks to Farrow, TheExcellentorators are going down for the count. I should be doing a happy dance right now. Except . . .

"It's notable for . . ."

I'm not sure what's happening. Or why. I'm suddenly leaning toward TheExcellentorators' performance space. *"For having a ninety-degree angle!"* I hiss. "The other two angles are different, but if you add them together, they equal a hundred and eighty degrees."

Farrow whips around to stare at me. He's not the only one. I must not have been as quiet as I'd hoped. Dr. Yee zeros in on me like a laser beam.

"Yay for audience participation!" I yell. "Great job planning ahead, TheExcellentorators. Woo-hoo!"

Farrow wipes his brow. "Yeah. Right. What he said! So, uh, the right triangle has never been completed successfully in front of a live Benjamin Banneker audience.

Friends and guests, this move requires all five members of our team to participate. One moment please. Once again, we will lie on the ground for this performance."

It looks like the plan is for Pixie and Farrow to be the leg of the triangle. Ritchie and JoJo are the base. LaVontay's the hypotenuse—the long, slanted line that connects the leg and the base.

"I shouldn't have had so many tacos at lunch," Ritchie moans. He gets no sympathy from the other TheExcellentorators. Farrow and Pixie roll him like a bowling ball until he's in the right spot. Then everyone but LaVontay slides into position.

LaVontay ballet-leaps to the middle of the invisible hypotenuse. The crowd starts to murmur.

"What's happening?"

"Should he be there?"

"I thought all ends of a triangle had to touch."

"First position!" LaVontay announces. He sticks his arms out for balance and stands with the heels of his feet together.

"Oooh!"

"I think he's going to do a ballet thing."

"Second position!" LaVontay slides his feet until they're about hip distance apart. "Splits!" He pastes a smile on his face and slowly, slowly, sloooowly slides his legs apart until his butt hits the ground. One of LaVontay's feet touches the top of the triangle's leg (a.k.a. Pixie's head). His other foot touches the tip of the base (a.k.a. Ritchie's foot).

Holy cow, they did it! They closed the triangle! "That's totally amazing!" Travis shouts.

Padgett does a happy dance in her sky-blue clogs. "Good job, TheExcellentorators!"

Most of them are happy.

"I think I need Coach Judy," Ritchie whimpers.

"I'm stuck," LaVontay says. "Could somebody call my mom?"

CHAPTER 35

Frederick Douglass Zezzmer

Last week, if anyone told me that I would clap for a sportster team, I would've said nope, you're wrong. Have you met any sportsters? But here I am, cheering as loud as anybody.

I'm not sure how Dr. Yee did it, but he got all of us celebrating for each other.

Farrow lines up his team up to wait for our performance. Well, most of his team. Ritchie really did hurl. He went to Coach Judy's office while the performance area got hosed down.

"Go, team!" Farrow yells. "Go, TravLiUeyPadgeyZezz!" Some things you have to see to believe.

When the field dries out, we walk to the center of the performance space to face Dr. Yee, The DOM, and the judges. I clasp my hands then shake them out. I do a couple of deep knee bends. I swivel my head. It's how I calm down before a big inventing challenge, but it doesn't help at all now.

I paste on a smile that's as stiff as LaVontay's just before he did the splits. I'm the one in front, closest to the bleachers. Everybody else is stationed so Huey doesn't have to be in the spotlight.

"B-B community," I shout. "We hope you enjoyed The-Excellentorators' performance. We sure did. Give it up for them one more time!" When the applause dies down, I wave my arm toward Huey, Padgett, Liam, and Travis. "To conclude this challenge, TravLiUeyPadgeyZezz will perform"—I gulp—"Photosynthesis: The Musical, with original songs and gesture-things we just created."

Travis squeals. She's so excited. That's one of us. I borrow Farrow's phrase: "One-two-three-GO!"

Travis throws her arms to the sky and sings:

I am a plant.
A plant is me.
Sittin' in the sun.
Waitin' for some fun.
Something photosynthesis-y.

Huey and Liam march around her. They move their arms back and forth like train rods and chant,

"Photosynthesis-Photosynthesis-Photosynthesis-Photo-synthesis."

I wish I had their parts. My face is starting to hurt from stiff-smiling.

"Magic happens during the photosynthesis process," I say. "The plant converts water, also known as H_2O, and carbon dioxide, also called CO_2, into what it needs to live."

Travis starts to bend and bow like one of those inflatable, pop-up balloons that Be Healthy Mart uses to get attention when they have a sale. She's really into it. Huey was right! We've got this. TravLiUeyPadgeyZezz is on fire!

Padgett makes huge, witchy, spell-casting gestures before she sings new words to "It's a Hard Knock Life" from *Annie.*

> *Li'l plant takes*
> *C-O-2*
>
> *And she takes*
> *some wa-ter, too.*
>
> *'lectrons scram from*
> *H-2-O*
>
> *Into C-O-2*
> *They*
> *Go.*

Now it's my turn! My mouth opens like it's supposed to but . . . the only words I remember are about the sides and angles of right triangles. *Oh no.* I forgot all the words to my song.

I look at Huey. "Um . . ." He stops walking. Liam bumps into him and almost falls. Padgett quits singing to help. Travis does her best to demonstrate photosynthesis through high-stomping and hopping, but she doesn't have backup vocals anymore. TravLiUeyPadgeyZezz is falling apart. It's all my fault. Everyone is watching me. All I can think of is how dumb I look. Now I know what Huey means about the stage fright ogre shouting in his ears. It's horrible. I try to kick into inventor Plan B mode, but there's nothing. For the first time ever, there's . . . nothing.

"As TheExcellentorators said, AND NOW A WORD FROM OUR SPONSOR!" It's Huey. He runs out of line and stands beside me. Huey hates this kind of attention, but if we were on a stage, we'd be in the spotlight together.

"What's going on?" Travis whispers to us from behind. Padgett looks furious. "What are you doing?"

"When did we change the script?" Liam asks.

"Oh man, I'm sorry! I forgot you helped Farrow," Huey whispers. "Take it easy. You'll remember the words in a minute. Like Grandpa said, 'Jest bests stress.' Watch the show."

What show?

Huey does a quick HueyLink pose. Then he yanks out his magic cards and jumps in front of me. Now he's alone in the spotlight. Everybody's watching him. He's so scared his whole body twitches. But, he doesn't stop. "A-a-attention, B-B audience. We're, um, we're going to take a break from our exciting presentation for an important announcement. Behold this deck of magic cards!"

He manages to make it through his first trick—somehow making all the cards turn white after one shuffle—without puking. Then, he calls some mathatrons up to count cards while he makes the deck go from 52 cards to 40 to 18 to ten with each shuffle. They watch him like hawks, but they can't figure it out. He gets through everything with no mistakes. When he's finished, I throw up my arms and start an avalanche of applause.

Huey bows. He's still twitching, but not so much anymore. He grins at me, stuffs his cards in his pocket and does a quick message in sign language: *Just figured out what Grandpa meant by 'say cheers to fears.' And once I started performing, it was okay.*

He doesn't mention that he only performed because I was in trouble big time.

"Wasn't that great?" I bellow. "And now, sit back for the conclusion of Photosynthesis: The Musical." *Funny.* I remember all the song words now.

Water becomes ox–y–gen,
CO_2 is glu–cose then.
It's the way things go!

Padgett and I harmonize on the next part. That means she sings extra loud to drown out my pitchiness.

Ms. Plant sends O
InTheAirForUs.
And pumps energy
Into glu–uuu–cose.

It'sSoCool. It'sSoAwesome.
Don't you luv it?

Ohhhhhhhhhhhhhhhh!
WHOAAAAAAAAAA!

Photo–syn–the–sis!

Technically, this is where I'm supposed to do another solo about how plants make themselves look green. But know what? I've done enough singing to last a lifetime.

I haiku–rap–lecture like a professor the rest of the photosynthesis process. For the record, thinking up words that rhyme with *chloroplasts* and *chlorophyll* is not easy. If this were a science test, I'd give myself an A.

When we finally finish, we're all hot and sweaty. Liam lets Travis sit on his shoulders. The crowd doesn't seem to care that we didn't do the whole thing in a song. They jump to their feet and cheer. Farrow whoops loudest of all.

"I can't believe we made it," I wheeze. "Sorry for forgetting my lines."

Padgett pats my back. "It's all good."

"Yeah. No worries," Liam says. "Team TravLiUey-PadgeyZezz forever!"

Travis gives an exhausted wave.

"Personally, I think the haiku-rap added flavor. I didn't know you could do that." Huey throws an arm across my shoulders. He makes a fist with his free hand and pops it out for a bump. "Yay, team?"

I bump back.

"Yay, team!"

And honestly, I'm probably grinning bigger than I've ever grinned when Dr. Yee and the judges step down to put the final punch in our punch cards.

At last!

CHAPTER 36

Destiny Octavia Moore (The DOM)

I hate public speaking.

It's terrified me ever since I stood in front of my sixth-grade class to deliver a report about why Ms. Katherine Johnson, Ms. Dorothy Vaughan, and Ms. Mary Jackson—three women who were instrumental in building America's space program—are my personal heroes. That was the first time many of my classmates learned that some of the most exceptional mathematicians, programmers, and scientists who were part of NASA's "human computer" team were women and Black. Not everyone believed me.

Everest Jackson snorted and made two big thumbs-down when I started listing the women's achievements. And when I finished, legs wobbly and hands shaking so hard I could barely hold the pages of my report, Kieran

O'Shaughnessy jumped up and shouted, "That's not true! You're a liar! You made the whole thing up!"

They were furious when Mrs. Ruben sent them to the principal's office, even though they'd both been there so many times already that the waiting bench should have had their names carved into it when they were in first grade.

And although I was *pretty* sure nothing bad would happen while I waited for the bus after school, I still would have been scared if my best friend, David Yee—yes, my math club buddy—hadn't skipped baseball practice and risked getting detention to wait with me.

Some people say they want to pretend middle school never happened. Not me. I don't want to forget. I know for a fact that middle school made me strong.

I suck in a breath, stomp my kicks, and pop my fists on my hips. I strike a superhero pose.

I waggle my fingers at David, giving the super-short version of the secret shake we did in math club. Then I whip around and grin at the kids. The brave, creative, awesome kids who faced challenges they weren't expecting, found encouragement from their school community, and managed to do amazing things.

Douglass waves at me from the bleachers. Padgett gives me a thumbs-up. So does Farrow. Even Ritchie lifts a hand. He's still looking a little green.

The rest of their teams smile anxiously.

I take another deep breath.

"Picking a winning team for this challenge was much harder than I imagined four days ago. I'm so proud of all of you," I say. "But Dr. Yee, the judges, and I promised that we would award the first-ever STEAMS trophy to the winning team. So that's what we're going to do. Team TheExcellentorators and Team TravLiUey-PadgeyZezz, please come forward."

Ten grubby kids trot back on the field. Team members high-five themselves. Then they high-five their competitors. Ritchie even high-fives Liam—a move David told me he was really hoping to see.

"After careful consideration and following a close review of all of the challenge points, the winning team is . . . TheExcellentorators!" I yell. "Everybody, give it up for the champs!"

Farrow lets out the loudest yell I've ever heard. Pixie and JoJo hug each other. LaVontay does an impressive spin on the grass. Ritchie manages to muster the energy for another thumbs-up.

TravLiUeyPadgeyZezz is downcast. I know what they're thinking: If this were a movie, we would have pulled out a win.

Travis Cod wipes her eyes. Liam Murphy kicks the grass. Padgett Babineaux flicks her retainer. Huey

Linkmeyer whips out his phone. From what David told me, he's probably looking for loopholes in the rules.

The rest of the students don't seem to know whether to cheer or boo, so they stay silent. Poor David. He had his hopes set on STEAMS teaching the kids that there's more to life than winning. But I guess some things can't be . . .

"Hey! Come on, you guys!" It's Douglass Zezzmer. He jumps up and down in front of his team. "We did so good! We finished sports and art and STEM competitions, and we didn't kill each other." He points at TheExcellentorators. "They were just better today. We can still be happy for them. We're all friends, right?" He waves his arms. "Give it up for the winners! *Ex-cel-lent. Ex-cel-lent. Ex-cel-len-tor-a-tors.*"

The other TravLiUeyPadgeyZezzers join in. "*They're supersmart. They're also strong.*"

Then the rest of the crowd, including David and including me, chimes in for the big finish. "*They're genius alligators.*"

"For the record, we totally would have beat you if we'd had a song," Douglass yells. He grins at Farrow. "Wait till next year!"

"You're on!" Farrow grins back. "But first, Team The-Excellentorators, let's hear it for the best competitors— and the best new friends—ever." He leads his team in a five-person wave for TravLiUeyPadgeyZezz. It spreads like fire. Soon everyone in the bleachers is doing it.

When that settles down, I shout the next accolade that David and I agreed on. "Now, let's hear it for the teachers, administrators, and judges who made this competition happen!"

There's another huge burst of applause. It blankets the field like a warm down comforter. Mr. Happy's cheeks turn pink. He blinks a little too fast and uses his fists to wipe his eyes. Mrs. Jalil beams. Ms. Latrice puts her hands over her heart. Coach Judy's smile is huge.

I wink at David. *You did it!* He shakes his head and mouths, "Not me."

He's wrong. Somebody should tell him.

So, I make the announcement he wasn't expecting.

"And now, everybody, let's hear it for Benjamin Banneker's most valuable team player, the person who believes everyone has potential, the person who dreamed up STEAMS and created this amazing competition . . . your wonderful principal, Dr. David Yee!"

As far as I know, David didn't get any applause in middle school.

Never.

Not ever.

Not one time.

And there were so many times he deserved it.

He almost drops his iPad in amazement when the students, teachers, administrators, and judges respond to my request.

The claps, the whoops, and the artsy kids' cheers of "Ho-ho. Hee-hee. Give it up for Dr. Yee!" are D-E-A-F-E-N-I-N-G!

CHAPTER 37

Frederick Douglass Zezzmer

f there was a contest for cooking up weekend chores to give kids when they're on punishment, Moms and Julius would totally win. *Clean the planters. Wash the windows. Hose out the trash cans. Turn the compost bins. Mow the lawn. Water the vegetables. Do the laundry. Sweep out Mr. Cohen's garage.* And that's just for starters.

I even have to rearrange the plastic owls that are supposed to keep squirrels out of the garden. For the record, city squirrels aren't dumb. They may have little rodent brains, but even they know plastic owls are fake. Which is why my next invention will be a solar-powered, motion-sensitive, animatronic owl that spreads its wings and snaps its beak and stalks through the garden following a programmed path. It'll blow those squirrels' teeny minds.

Huey wanted to help me with my chores, but he's busy. He's—wait for it—doing a show for all of the Porch View residents. His parents and steps are all going to watch him. He's going to be great. His parents are going to send me a video so I can see everything.

I'm getting ready to check the trellises that are supposed to keep the blueberry bushes from spreading across the patio when the back door bangs open. Pops stalks out. His legs are stiff. His back is rigid. He's acting like Barack Opawsma does when he sees another cat on TV.

I get it. After getting an earful from Moms about "effective hands-on parenting," it couldn't have been easy for Pops to schedule a time to visit me when both Moms and Julius were home. He's got to hate having them watch us like hawks from the kitchen window.

I give him a little wave.

Pops nods but doesn't wave back. He's not doing the EZ stare. Not exactly. But he still looks like he's about to explode. He walks right up to me, then crouches down until his nose is an inch from my face.

"How much do you know about my football career, Doug?"

My brain goes blank. We're not singing, but I still feel like I'm having another bout of mondegreen. "Uh . . ."

"Yeah, that's what I thought." Pops straightens up and pops his hands on his hips HueyLink-style. "Listen, I'm going to say this fast, son. It's not something I tell many folks. When I . . ." He clears his throat longer than I've ever heard anyone clear their throat in my life. "When I first started playing football in high school, I wasn't very good. I spent a lot of time on the bench my first year. It was hard. But that's when I decided to train more and do everything I could to be the best. No more riding the bench. I was going to be a starter at everything. For the rest of my life. Football taught me that. Do you understand what I'm saying?"

Having a conversation like this with Pops is worse than being in a musical. My pits are sweating. I'm fast-blinking. I seriously want to lie down. But I don't lie. I shake my head. "No."

"What I'm saying is . . ." Pops stops. He tries again. "What I'm saying is, our problem is that you don't see me as your starter father. That's why all of this talk about being an inventor instead of doing sports really bothers me." He shrugs. "That's what your mother thinks, anyway."

Pops clears his throat again. Shorter this time. "It's easy enough to fix. We'll spend more time together. Maybe we can, uh . . ." He looks around our yard like he hopes an idea will pop out of one of the plants. Then his gaze hits my workshop. He looks away fast. "Maybe we can watch sports at my house and do pick-up games on the weekends. That will be our time. Just your brother and us."

He swivels side to side. I've seen enough video of him on YouTube to know that this is his post-game cooldown. He's pretty sure we're done.

He doesn't know that fireworks are going off in my stomach. He made another plan. And he didn't even ask me. Again! I kick the pile of mulch I'd raked up before he got here and send it flying.

The screen door bangs open right away. Julius and Moms trot down the gravel path. They don't run, but . . . they get here really fast. They stand on either side of me. Julius's big arm drapes across my shoulders. "Everything okay out here?" he rumbles.

"We're good," Pops says. He glues his eyes on Moms. "I was just explaining how things are going to be and Doug got a little excited. No cause for alarm."

"Doug?" Moms asks.

I shake my head. Moms says my problem with Pops is about more than sports or inventing. Maybe she's right.

I glare up at Pops. He takes a step back. Whoa—I think I launched my version of the EZ stare.

"Looks like Doug has something to say," Pops says. He waves his hand between him and Moms. "I think it should be a conversation with the original parents." He narrows his eyes at Julius. His words are like an end-of-class bell. Julius is being dismissed. We all know it.

Julius sighs. "I'll be right inside."

The fireworks in my stomach turn into a meteor strike.

"You should stay," Moms says. "We're *all* parents here."

Pops shakes his head. "No, no, no. Doug is old enough to know who his parents are. And he thinks . . ."

"I want Julius to stay," I blurt.

Everything goes silent. Even the birds know something's up. They stop chirping. That's huge. They've been noisy all day.

The smell of Julius's *mystery meat meatloaf with don't ask me why it's green sauce* pours through the window. My mouth starts watering.

It's weird timing.

But also, kind of not.

Now I understand why Moms and Julius agreed to CCCP. I don't want keep fighting. There's not a kid-version of CCCP, though, so I rush over and give Pops a hug. It's not what he's expecting. He's stiff as a robot.

"You'll always be my starter pops," I tell him. "No matter what. You know what I'm saying?"

"Yes. Sure. Of course. I know that." I wonder how Pops's stomach is doing. He's breathing really hard.

I step back. "But you want to be my pops *and* my dad. And . . . I'm sorry, but you can't. I already have a dad. *Julius* is my dad. He's been my dad for as long as I can remember. And, like you always say, there's no such thing as an ex-parent."

I walk back to Julius. His arm drops across my shoulders. Like I said, he's predictable.

"You weren't here most of my life, Pops. I'm glad you are now, but while you were gone Julius taught me to ride a bicycle." I'm getting a case of Huey's stage fright. My voice is shaking. So is the rest of me. "He helps me with inventing. He goes to all my school programs. He cried when I broke my arm skateboarding and the doctors had to set it. He grounds me when I get in trouble. He's teaching me to shave."

Moms's eyebrows shoot up. Julius shrugs. I think he's trying to sound cool, but his voice shakes a little. "Boy's growing up, Annie. Depending on the day, he almost has a whisker."

"I'm really glad you came back to Denver, Pops. And I'm really proud of you. I want to do more stuff together so we get to know each other." I suck in a breath. "But I'm not giving up my time with Julius. And I don't like it when you pretend he doesn't matter, Pops. I want you to stop."

Julius's arm trembles on my shoulders. Pops's mouth drops open. He looks like he wants to say something, but can't figure out the right words. He wipes sweat from his forehead.

"I don't . . ." Pops looks at me. His eyes are shiny. "Do I . . ." He looks at Moms and Julius. "Whoa." He looks at me again. "You've been holding that in?" When I nod, he asks, "Anything else?"

"Well, yeah. I have my own plan for my life, Pops." My voice isn't shaking anymore. I think my pits are drying out, too. Grandpa Linkmeyer's advice works like Huey said. Now that I'm started, I'm okay. "I'm going to be an inventor. The World's Greatest Inventor. I'm not doing pro sports."

Pops sighs. "I hear you." He looks me in the eye. "I may not have been the best listener in the past, but . . . I'm listening now." He smiles at Julius. His teeth show this time. "This dad thing isn't something you can learn from books or classes or the internet, is it?"

Julius shakes his head. "It most certainly is not."

"Maybe you could give me some pointers. We could talk at an Avalanche game. Do you like hockey? I can get tickets."

For the record, Julius does not like hockey. He nods anyway. "Thanks, Elliott. That would be great."

Huh. Last week, all I wanted was to win STEAMS and get picked for GadgetCon. I didn't win. I didn't get picked. But I helped T.W. with his paper. I rescued Farrow when he had trouble with his presentation. Huey rescued me when I had trouble with mine. I made a bunch of new friends. All my parents are talking. And I think I may have a brother now.

I didn't get any of the stuff I thought I wanted. But, I'm still happy.

It's kind of weird things worked out this way.

But then again, kind of not.

CHAPTER 38

Dr. Yee

To: Ann Z. Jordan, Julius Jordan, Elliott Zezzmer
From: David Yee, Ph.D.

Good morning, parents and guardians!

It's been two weeks since the end of our inaugural STEAMS competition. I want to take a moment to express my gratitude, once again, for Douglass's performance during and after the contest. I trust you're proud of him. I certainly am.

I also want to share some exciting news about Rocky Mountain GadgetCon. While I certainly understand—and support—your decision to decline my invitation for Douglass to represent Benjamin Banneker at GadgetCon this summer, I recently learned that GadgetCon will host a new event in the fall.

I have high hopes for Benjamin Banneker at that event! I hope you will consider allowing Douglass to participate. I have always been impressed with his abilities as an inventor, but the maturity and leadership he demonstrated at STEAMS convinced me that he is ready to join our older students in the quest for a prestigious GadgetCon medal.

By the way, if any of you would be willing to help judge GadgetCon's fall competition, please let me know. Adult supervision is *always* appreciated. I will send details to anyone who is interested. (If you do attend, be sure to wear long-sleeve shirts, long pants, and running shoes to the event. Fireproof jumpsuits will be provided on-site.)

Fall GadgetCon will take place at the Colorado Convention Center in late October. Students will spend their entire fall break preparing. It won't be easy, but it will be a wonderful experience for someone who, I have no doubt, will one day be known as the World's Greatest Inventor!

Best Regards,

David Yee

CHAPTER 39

Mrs. Jalil

To: Terrell Wallace Jackson-Zezzmer
From: Mrs. Jalil, Assistant Principal

Dear Terrell,

Thank you again for calling to explain what happened with your application essay. It's a very brave person who admits when he's wrong.

I'm pleased that you understand how important it is to do your own work in classes. That said, I'm delighted to hear that you rewrote your report on Shakespeare, submitted it on time, and received an A+. Bravo!

I appreciate you sending your paper to me so I could read it. I was impressed by your thoughtful critique. You have an impressive mind. You should trust your instincts more often.

I also appreciate you being up-front about using your stepbrother's DougApp technology to help organize your paper. As you no doubt know, we approved DougApp's use in this area for another student.

What you may not know is that your stepbrother asked me to reconsider your application. Apparently, he thinks you would make outstanding contributions to our school. Your mother, your guidance counselor, and your current teachers agree. Your stepfather also believes you have much to offer Benjamin Banneker— but, as you know, he has many concerns about the robustness of our sports programs. However, he graciously volunteered to help with our high school athletic teams. He spent several hours with Coach Judy sharing his ideas. She remains speechless with delight.

But back to the purpose of this letter.

After careful consideration, and following several long talks with our principal, I'm thrilled to inform you that you have been accepted to Benjamin Banneker for the coming school year!

Do not worry about entering tenth grade without knowing anyone. One of Douglass's TravLiUey-PadgeyZezz teammates has tested out of middle school and into your class. Her name is Travis

Elizabeth Cod. Perhaps you can meet with her this summer, after she returns from astronaut camp in California, to get another perspective about our school.

Welcome to B-B, T.W.! We're looking forward to seeing you next August.

Have a wonderful summer!

Mrs. Jalil

Acknowledgments

I knew I wanted to be an author in grade school. I will always be grateful to those who recognized and encouraged that dream.

Three women were particularly supportive. My high school English teacher, Mrs. Helen Yeager, saw writing as art. She did much more than grade my assignments. She noticed the joy I got from reading and writing, recommended additional books to keep the spark going, and encouraged me to continue to write.

I only met Nichelle Nichols—*Star Trek's* original Uhura—once, but that experience was transformative. I attended a Star Trek convention as a college newspaper reporter. Painfully shy, I lurked by the door until Ms. Nichols spotted me. She said, "I see you. Don't stay in the back." Then she brought me to the front of the room to sit with the cast. I don't think I managed to gasp out a single question, but I will always remember hearing, "I see you."

Laura Pegram, the founder and executive director of Kweli, has dedicated years and years to helping aspiring authors connect with the agents or editors most likely to be receptive to their art. The care she took with my submission led me to my dream publisher, Levine Querido.

And speaking of Levine Querido, I couldn't ask for a better literary home. Arthur Levine championed adding diverse voices to publishing long before there was a thing called social media. He's built a publishing house that is celebrated, productive, nurturing, and inclusive. I'm honored to be part of it.

There aren't enough words in any language, real or fictional, to adequately thank the incomparable Nick Thomas, LQ's executive editor. Nick, you've been my coach, mentor, cheerleader, and advocate throughout this process. Your advice and edits made this book stronger with each revision. Thank you, friend! I'm so fortunate to work with you. I can't wait to start book #2.

LQ's marketing and publicity team of Antonio Gonzalez Cerna and Irene Vázquez continue to amaze me. You are fantastic-extraordinary-awesome-amazing communication pros. You're simply the best. Thank you both for all you do!

Filip Peraić, designing *Control Freaks's* book cover wasn't just a job to you. You read the manuscript from first word to last, immersed yourself in the world of Benjamin Banneker College Prep, and discovered the essence of Doug Zezzmer. Your empathy and artistry are evident in the amazing cover that you created. Thank you so much!

From the wonderful chapter icons created for each character to figuring out the challenges for formatting backwards text and 51 wacky team names, Semadar Megged's creativity and page design wizardry made *Control Freaks* a thing of beauty. Thank you, Semadar!

From the beginning, my agent, Quressa Robinson at Folio, has been a quiet warrior, expertly navigating the realities of the publishing business with the sometimes unrealistic dreams of a debut author. I'm incredibly lucky to have you in my corner, Quressa.

My writing buddy, Carleen Brice, is both a fantastic author and wonderful friend. *Control Freaks* might still be a work-in-progress were it not for those 6 A.M. texts of, "Ready to write? Let's go!" Grab a cup of coffee, Carleen. We have more writing to do!

The 2023DebutSistars—Autumn Allen, Kaija Langley, Rhonda Roumani and Khadijah VanBrankle—are proof that women supporting each other generate phenomenal positive energy. Cheering each other's successes and bolstering each other's spirits when we were low are memories that I will cherish forever. Cheers, Sistars! I can't wait to read your books.

Kweli, Lighthouse Writers, and Highlights Foundation are cornerstones in my writing community. Kweli's workshops and conferences helped me transition from writing to storytelling, and the network of friends I made there provided sanctuary when I needed it. Thank you, Laura and team.

Lighthouse Writers: Andrea Dupree, you sprang into action following my first, "Uh . . . what do I do now?" email. Thank you so much! And thank you to my Lighthouse Book Project mentor, the amazing author, Eleanor Brown, and to the instructors who helped improve my craft over the years: Victoria Hanley, William Haywood Henderson, Lisa Kennedy, Erika Krouse, Sarah Elizabeth Schantz, and Mathangi Subramanian.

Highlights Foundation's Craft, Community and Your Career 10-month program was quite a commitment, and every moment was worthwhile. I'm grateful for the lessons learned and the writing colleagues met. Chris Tebbetts, you shared knowledge and insight with grace and generosity. You are a mighty, mighty wordsmith, an excellent instructor, and an all-around good person. Thank you!

I also benefited from the work of the dedicated staffs at Authors Guild, Margins and SCBWI. Please know that every action you take to support writers is recognized and appreciated.

Thank you to my immediate and extended family, my new and long-time friends, and my wonderful pals at Kent Denver School. Talk about a cheer squad. I appreciate you!

Last but definitely not least, thank you to my husband, Elbert, who threw himself into bookstore visits and "you've got this" speeches with all the determination of the retired U.S. Marine that he is. What a ride we've had! Love always, Jan.

P.S.: Inez J. Thomas and Jamal Edwards, keep writing. The world needs your books.

J.E. Thomas grew up near Colorado's Front Range
mountains. She spent her early summers stuffing grocery
bags with books at the local library, reading feverishly, then
repeating the process week after week. J.E. has bachelor's
degrees in Mass Communications and Political Science, as
well as a master's degree in Public Communications. She
wrote *Control Freaks* while working as an administrator at
the same independent school she attended as child.

The jacket and case were designed by Filip Peraić using pencils in the concept stage, then Adobe Illustrator and Procreate for the final art. The text was set by Westchester Publishing Services, in Danbury, CT, in Adobe Caslon Pro, a revival of 18th-century English typefounder William Caslon's work, designed by Carol Twombly. Known for its practicality, Caslon was used for the first printings of the American Declaration of Independence and the Constitution. The display was set in Futura, a geometric sans serif designed by German Paul Renner for the Bauer Type Foundry in 1927. The book was printed on 78 gsm Yunshidai Ivory uncoated woodfree FSC™-certified paper and bound in China.

Production supervised by Freesia Blizard
Book interiors designed by Semadar Megged
Editor: Nick Thomas
Assistant Editor: Irene Vázquez

LQ